THE BAD KIND OF LUCKY

Also by **Matt Phillips**

THREE KINDS OF FOOL
ACCIDENTAL OUTLAWS
REDBONE
BAD LUCK CITY

THE
BAD
KIND OF
LUCKY

MATT PHILLIPS

SHOTGUN
HONEY
SHOTGUNHONEYBOOKS.COM

The Bad Kind of Lucky
Text copyright © 2018 Matt Phillips

Published by Shotgun Honey, an imprint of Down & Out Books

Shotgun Honey
PO Box 75272
Charleston, WV 25375
www.ShotgunHoney.com

Down & Out Books
3959 Van Dyke Rd, Ste. 265
Lutz, FL 33558
www.DownAndOutBooks.com

Cover Design by Bad Fido.

First Printing 2018

ISBN-10: 1-64396-002-4
ISBN-13: 978-1-64396-002-9

May you always be on the run.

THE BAD KIND OF LUCKY

1

REMMIE MIKEN HEARD THE VOICES through the wall, two loud-mouths shouting at each other in the studio apartment next door. Something about a skinny girl named Veranda and a used Dodge Charger with low miles. Remmie caught bits and pieces, put together that the girl was gone, but somehow the Dodge might still be around, maybe in Tijuana. Who-fucking-knew?

Thing was: Remmie couldn't sleep.

Not with the shouting and the stomping and the constant back and forth about the goddamn car. Whether the girl and the car were in Tijuana or not, Remmie was tired after ten hours on fryer duty at Big Stop's Roadhouse, a grease pit burger joint smudged beneath a freeway overpass on the outskirts of downtown. He worked six days a week and all he wanted—besides a timely fucking paycheck—was a few hours sleep before his next shift.

How to get some quiet in this rundown apartment

building?

He started by banging his fist against the wall and smothering himself with a lumpy pillow.

The conversation coming through the wall was the scumbag version of the scientific method:

Could be the girl got picked up by the cops, no? Would have been out by now, that's right. Okay, so she didn't get picked up, but maybe the girl took the Dodge up north? What'd the raspy-voiced guy think? Well, he thought the skinny bitch was too lazy to drive herself. No, she maybe sold the car to a gringo down on the border, used the money for a flight to Mexico City. The Dodge had leather interior, a decent sound system. Some nice fucking rims.

Big loss. Too big. They had to find it. And Veranda, too.

This fucking car. This fucking skinny girl who runs off without a word. Remmie wanted to burn the car and kill the girl, drown these two loudmouths in their own toilet bowl. He tried some deep breathing exercises, a thing he learned in his anger management courses—it was no good.

He couldn't fucking sleep.

He got out of bed and put his ear to the wall. He noticed how bare his apartment looked. Sad. Pitiful, in fact. All he had in the place was a mattress on the floor, a cell phone plugged into the wall, and a mini-fridge filled with cheap beer next to the electric stove. He had a stack of paperback books, too. Old mysteries he found in a cardboard box in the alley outside his apartment building. Moody covers. Tough guys with five o'clock shadow and loaded pistols. Naked women clutching wet sheets in dingy motel rooms.

For all Remmie knew, the books could have belonged to the skinny girl.

He listened while the two men talked:

"Veranda couldn't find her own reflection in a mirror."

The raspy voice said, "Trust me, that girl knows what kind of money Leo Action pulls in. Don't think she doesn't have the balls to rip him off."

"If she took the car, she did it because it was easy. That's all."

"Fuck if I believe that. She's smarter than you give her credit for."

"She didn't know about the cop."

More from raspy voice, "She does now."

"Maybe, maybe not."

Remmie banged on the wall again and said, "Can you two shut the fuck up? I'm trying to sleep over here." Before he could scream at them again, a blast slammed his ears and Remmie stumbled backwards, sat on the cheap carpet. It was like being shot through a cloud; he didn't know what was happening. His ears rang and pain started in the front of his head. What the fuck? He wiped particles of dry wall from his face, brushed dust off his hands and arms. He squinted through the darkness, tried to stand up, fell onto his knees. After a few deep breaths, Remmie stood and stared at a gaping crevice in the wall, just below where it met the ceiling; it looked like his apartment was yawning. He could see the two-by-four wall studs and some red and green electrical wires dangling through the slit. Across the room, in the far wall, he saw the splattered, pockmarked surface of a shotgun blast.

Those scumbag motherfuckers: They shot a hole in his wall.

Looked like Remmie needed to pay his neighbors a visit.

● ● ●

Remmie Miken was starting over after a bad run.

Divorce.

Lost custody.

Ten thousand dollars in gambling debt.

Here's a bit of advice: Know what the fuck cricket is before you start laying bets on the sport—it's a hell of a lot more complicated than you think.

What happened to Remmie could—he was sure—happen to almost any high school graduate. You start out alright, but you get bored. You get sick of frying catfish and mixing mayonnaise into tarter sauce. Everything starts to feel watered down; your snot-nosed kid cries a little too long each night, your wife asks a few too many questions, and your mother-in-law won't stop talking about Oprah and her favorite reality tv shows. The double-wide starts to feel too much like a cell in the county jail.

Next thing you know, you're sipping from a toilet bowl in a dive bar down by the mud flats, a thick slab of hand holding you by the neck.

Here's the gist: They want their fucking money.

Of course, later, there's a whole arson plot when it comes to the double-wide. And insurance fraud. Too much bail money to think about. And collateral, what little you have. Another bit of advice: Those class rings aren't worth a solid-shitty-half of what you paid for them. Oh, and they're not real gold either.

Just so you know, you know?

Point is, Remmie Miken needed a fresh start after the first thirty-six years of his life. He thought he'd try to make it in the Big City. Give it the old junior college try. Why not? All his shit was burned up and he'd never been loved.

Not for what he was, at least.

How much worse could life get?

● ● ●

The apartment building was low-rent, a two-story place next to a freeway on-ramp, refurbished with cheap carpet and mismatched paint. No credit check required. The property manager told Remmie not to cook meth or grow marijuana. Everything else, from Remmie's experience in the building, was fair game. That included prostitution—the skinny girl's vocation.

Funny, Veranda was taking a vacation from her vocation.

Rolling around TJ in a stolen Dodge Charger.

Not a bad way to do it if you asked Remmie. He rode the city bus to work and thinking about it made him want to scream. Anyway, he was used to living with scum. Hell, he was used to living in scum. But Remmie needed sleep; he needed it so he could go back to making limp-dick French fries in the morning. And these scumbags next door would not shut the fuck up—there was also the new decorating they'd done to his apartment. Remmie didn't have a gun, not yet. The best he could find was a butter knife with a bent tip. He carried it in his right hand as he walked down the hall. He reached the next door apartment and pounded on the loose number seven nailed to the door. "What the fuck, man? I need to talk to you guys. I have to work in the morning and—"

The door swung open and Remmie gasped. His voice lodged in his throat and a headache burned behind his eyes. In front of him, face speckled with blood, was a fat man with a shotgun propped on one shoulder. He smiled at Remmie— the man's top two front teeth were missing—and said, "Nice to see you, neighbor. I could use a little help with the clean up over here. Thanks for the visit." The fat man moved aside and waved Remmie into the room. "Come on in. Hurry on in. Don't stand out there like a stranger. Let's be friends."

Remmie slipped the butter knife into a pocket.

He shuffled into the apartment.

So much for starting a new life. Remmie had an odd feeling, a feeling like he was slipping out of his new skin and back into his old one.

2

"NOW, YOU SEE HERE WHAT HAPPENS when I get annoyed?" The fat man pointed at the body draped across the carpet. "And sometimes, you know, when I get annoyed, people get in the way and, shit—" He grunted and cleared his throat. "They get some bad luck coming their way." The fat man jabbed the shotgun at Remmie; his cheeks flapped while he talked. "You the one banging on the goddamn wall? What do I have to do to have a decent business meeting in this shit hole? Here I am, in quiet palaver with my steamed colleague, and I got a fry cook," the fat man squinted at Remmie's ketchup-soiled pants, "thinking he's the goddam quiet-police. You got a badge to go with that righteous dig-nation? Or maybe you think everybody keeps the same hours as a broke-ass hamburger jockey? Is that it, friend?"

Remmie didn't know where to look.

He had two choices: The shotgun or the dead man.

The body was oddly twisted across the carpet, as if the

man—in blue-tinged pimp suit and wingtips—was doing ballet when he got plugged. Half his face, framed in dark oily curls, was drenched in blood; one eye was a fleshy black mass, like a tumor unveiled. From the looks of it, Mr. Pimp (raspy voice, Remmie knew by now) got half the load, and the other half plunged through the wall. A little more demo and they'd have a two-bedroom on their hands.

The fat man sighed. "What do you call yourself? What's your Christian name, friend?" He wagged the shotgun at Remmie. It was a finger of doom.

Remmie grunted, felt his throat tighten. He choked out a response. "Remmie. Miken. I live in number five, just down—"

"Howdy, neighbor. It's nice to meet you." He swung the shotgun toward the dead man, pumped it once, and fired. The blast filled the room, echoed like a heavy metal chord. The body shook with the gut shot. "One for fun," the fat man said turning back to Remmie. He tossed the gun onto a worn leather sofa. "They call me Trevor Spends around here." He smiled and offered Remmie a hand. "Because, like the name says, I spend."

Remmie forced himself to shake Trevor's hand. "Shit, I didn't know, I mean—fuck. I didn't figure you'd shoot the guy." Remmie rubbed the place between his eyes, tried to scrub away the pain. His ears rang; a sharp, persistent odor of gunfire filled his nose.

Trevor shrugged, pointed his palms at the ceiling. "Accidents happen, especially when I get pissed off. It's a weakness, I admit it." He looked into the dead space behind Remmie, as if conjuring a wise thought: "I got this therapist, guy says I shoot myself in the foot. You believe that? Says I let my anger run loose, like it's a rabid dog or something. I shoot myself in the foot, he says." Trevor laughed from the round fat belly beneath his suit and tie; he wore a blood-red tie over a black shirt—smart looking guy, even with the extra weight on him. "What I want to tell the guy, it's that I might shoot myself in the foot, but I'd like to shoot him in the throat. Right here," he said and lifted a finger to his Adam's apple. He lifted his eyebrows and smirked. "But I digress, huh?"

Remmie said, "You got blood on your face."

"Oh, shit. Give me a minute." Trevor went into the bathroom adjacent to the couch, just beyond the lifeless pimp. He ran the sink and scrubbed his face with a wet towel while Remmie stared at the scene. "You know, I didn't really care for Donny anyhow. He's the son of a bitch who let Veranda run off, take the fucking Dodge Charger with her. I let a guy borrow my car, and look what fucking happens, will you? Motherfucker brought it on his damn self."

Remmie lifted his eyes from the body, traced the shape of the shotgun on the couch. If he moved fast, he could have it in his hands before Trevor finished in the bathroom. One quick step, lift the goddamn thing, point it. But wait. No, two shots fired and that meant, what? Time to reload. Fuck. Okay, Remmie. You're going to walk out of here, let this scene be what it is. You're going to walk back to your apartment, crawl into bed, and sleep. That's what you're going to do—you're going to sleep. And when you wake up, this'll be so far away it never happened.

No dead pimps. No missing whores.

And, most of all, no fat man scrubbing blood off his face.

Except, no—you're going to stand here, Remmie. You'll wait.

Trevor came out of the bathroom, wiped the back of his neck with a blue towel. Blood ran down one side of the towel, like shit stains on boxer briefs. "Remmie, my new friend," he said, "how'd you like to make a little money?"

Too late, Remmie. You're stuck. "Doing what?"

Trevor lowered his chin at the dead pimp. "Well, now we got to chop him up, toss his ass in a dumpster somewhere. What do you say? There's five hundred big ones in it for you. And a nice breakfast when we finish."

Remmie licked his lips. He realized the pain in his head was gone, vanished behind dollar signs. He sniffed the air, scratched behind his head.

Without blinking, Remmie said: "Cut him up into how many pieces?"

3

TEN PIECES. THAT'S HOW MANY. Two each for the skinny arms. Two each for the legs, sawed through below the knobby knees. But you leave the torso all by itself after you cut the head off; Remmie never forgot how those dark curls looked rolling across the bathroom tile. *Jeez-us Kee-rist*. Trevor used a hacksaw to do the job, made Remmie watch. He leaned against the doorway, grimaced as his stomach knotted, tightened, released each time another body part came loose. Less bloody than Remmie imagined, but surreal as all hell. Trevor worked the saw like a carpenter, like he'd been doing it his whole life.

As he went through the second leg: "I don't expect you to do the dirty stuff, neighbor. But, hell, you got us into this." He stopped the slicing motion of the saw and looked over his shoulder at Remmie. His brown eyes looked both alive and dead at the same time. "And that means you got to be along for the ride. The whole ride, too. Not just the tossing the bags in the dumpster stuff. I'm talking the grunt work here." Trevor turned back to the body with an agonized grunt, bore down on the saw.

Kee-rist, Remmie thought again. The sound made his teeth grind: Ceaseless scraping mixed with the wet tearing of skin and flesh. Remmie said nothing. He tried to watch without watching, took in the rundown bathroom with its broken floor tiles (like a shitty subway station) and dirty bathtub, red streaks thickening by the second across chipped porcelain. Remmie worked once—for a long hellish week— in a butchering factory. They did pigs there. Remmie's job was to pull out the guts, plop them down on a conveyor belt. Five straight days, one fat pig after another, and Remmie woke up on his first day off with an unmistakable urge to slice his own throat. He quit the next day, didn't show up for work at the factory. His wife didn't like that decision, but that wasn't the worst of it—Remmie could never stomach bacon again.

Trevor finished the second leg, tossed the pieces at the foot of the bathtub. He shifted to the dead pimp's head. The body was draped over the tub, the pimp's neck lifted at the sky, his half-hairy chin pointed at the drab yellow lights and black mold sporing across the ceiling. "The thing with the head," Trevor said, "is that it comes away kind of messy, but it's an easy job. That's why I save it for last—you don't want to get messy before you have to. I bet you'll agree with me there, huh?" He positioned the hacksaw slightly higher than the pimp's Adam's apple. Before slicing, he stopped, turned to Remmie. "Know what? I could use an apron. Last thing I need is my dry-cleaning guy giving me a bunch of shit about a little blood. You mind?"

Remmie wandered like a ghost into the kitchen, opened a few drawers, found an apron crushed into a crusty ball. He walked back to the bathroom and handed it to Trevor. The fat man set the hacksaw on the edge of the sink and slipped the apron over his barbered hair, tied it around his broad belly. On the front of the apron was a cartoon image of a slim woman in a red bathing suit.

Trevor smoothed down the apron and studied his profile in the bathroom mirror. The glass was rutted with toothpaste stains and caked with the gunk of the dead pimp's uncouth and sporadic grooming habits. In the glass, Trevor was a lumpy shape framed by soap scum. He turned to face himself, ran his hands over the woman's curves. "Kiss this cook," Trevor said. He looked back at Remmie, noted the ketchup-stained pants again, and the greasy sheen of Remmie's boots. "Say, where in the hell do you work, neighbor? I bet I might know the place."

"Big Stop's Roadhouse. Just off the highway. We got—"

"The world's only egg-six-ways burger," Trevor said nodding his head.

"You know it?"

"Like the underside of my dick. I get the bacon burger with scrambled eggs on top. That's one hell of a meal, if you ask me."

Remmie said, "I bet I've cooked you a burger."

"It's a small world, neighbor."

Remmie glanced at the pimp's limbs piled in the tub. He'd come all this way—from the podunk shit heel town of his birth, from the mustard-odor of a dog food factory during the pitiful years of his youth, from the trailer park wedding and home births of his two little boys, from the county jail lockup—and wound up a fry cook at an inner city burger joint, a grease monkey standing in a shitty bathroom while a fat man in a suit chopped up a dead pimp.

Small world?

Yeah, Remmie guessed that about matched.

He said, "The smallest world."

Trevor picked up the hacksaw, drew it down across the dead pimp's neck, and began his bloody work. When it came free, the pimp's head dropped, bounced, and rolled casually across the tile floor. It ended up at Remmie's feet, the dead man's sky-blue eyes glaring up at him from the oily frame of black curls. Jeez-us, Remmie thought again. *Kee-rist.*

Trevor tossed the saw in the tub. "Time to bag this sucker up," he said. "This is where you're going to earn your money, neighbor."

"Jeez-us," Remmie said. "Kee-rist."

Trevor nodded and said, "Amen, brother. And may he rest in peace."

4

TRY AND CARRY A BAG OF PIMP'S LIMBS down two flights of stairs. See if you don't throw up all over yourself. What happens is you start to get short of breath and the smell of flesh and blood overwhelms the apartment building's normal piss and breastmilk stench; after a few steps you're thinking that midday cheeseburger and nacho fry plate were bad choices.

Remmie stopped on the landing between the first and second floors and tried to swing his heavy black trash bag—lumpy and wet with arms and legs—to his other shoulder. Trevor bumped into him from behind and Remmie teetered atop the steps, lost his grip on the bag and dropped it. He tried to hold back his vomit while the black Hefty plopped from one step to the next, a misshapen and ominous slinky. Remmie huffed down beef flavor and said, "Holy fuck."

The bag reached the bottom of the staircase and crashed into an aluminum trash bin, sent a clang through the building's hallways.

Trevor said, "Rookie mistake, goddammit."

An old man shuffled into view at the bottom of the steps. He ran a shaky hand through his frayed white hair. "What in the hell is this?"

Remmie took the steps two at a time, cleared his throat with authority when he reached the first floor, and said, "That's my stuff there, Mr. Noah. I'm just moving it over to a friend's place." He nodded at Trevor coming down the steps, "This is an associate of mine."

Mr. Noah grimaced at Trevor. He looked back at Remmie and said, "Well, what in the fuck are you throwing it at me for?"

"It was an accident, I lost my—"

"Fucking disrespect," Mr. Noah said. "That's what it is. This building used to be full of working people, not burnouts like you." He looked to Trevor, noticed the trim suit and tie. The old man's eyebrows hit his hairline. "Looks like you got a funeral to make, huh?" He waited for a response.

Trevor sighed. His eyes shot to Remmie, back to the expectant old man. "At least one funeral, Sparky. God knows I don't want to have to see another." He rolled his tongue against his left cheek, moved the black Hefty bag—pimp head and pimp torso—across his shoulders.

Mr. Noah looked from Trevor to Remmie. His mouth moved up and down the way it does on people prone to ample whiskey inhalation and ceaseless poker debt. He placed a shaky hand over his cue ball eyes, blindfolded himself. "Don't let me hold you up. I wouldn't want to get in the way of a good funeral."

Remmie lifted his bag, fell forward as Trevor shoved him into evening's inkwell light. He staggered, caught himself, marched onward with the severed limbs bumping against his ribcage.

Back in the stairwell, he heard the old man:

"Too few funerals in this damn city…"

• • •

…And Trevor was saying, "Neighborhoods like this, used to be you could kill a man and get rid of him in peace. I'll tell you what the problem is: It's gentrification. Beautification. Excavation…of the goddamn soul. That's what."

Remmie tightened his seatbelt as Trevor steered the car—a late '80s Mustang, black with tinted windows and mismatched rims—into a hard, right-angle turn. The tires squealed and the bags in the trunk bumped from one side to the other. The car sped along a main street headed in the general direction of downtown. As they gained speed, Remmie tried to catch the names on the brick-sided buildings. He saw 'Lavandería Azteca,' 'Pan de Maria,' 'Camisas y Pantalones…' Remmie might be a country boy in the deepest recesses of his soul, but he knew gentrification when he saw it—this was a far cry from that. What Remmie saw was a whole bunch of people trying to make it in this life, a whole bunch of poor suckers trying to hustle pennies for the rent man.

Trevor gripped the wheel with both hands, seemed to fill the whole car with his voice and fat and wrinkled, sweaty brow. "I remember when this was all eye-talian, get you a decent gnocchi on one corner and a gelato on the next. Make your girl cream her pants with a nickel and a kiss. Now, it's all pass-o-lay and tacos. Dios-fucking-mío, neighbor. We let the wrong ones in." He pointed at a tire shop, its steel bay doors pulled down and locked tight with chains and padlocks. "Used to be a bar there my uncle ran, place called DeMille's Dive. Hell of a place." Trevor whipped the car left across an unprotected intersection. Remmie grunted with the G-force. They raced at preposterous speed through a rundown residential neighborhood. Trevor kept on with his chatter and said, "They had a pool table in there and you had to put a dime on the table if you wanted to play. Buddy of mine, guy named Leo, went and made up fake dimes in the high school wood shop. Cut these fuckers real thin and painted 'em silver. Made notches all around the outside. Got us about a hundred free games of pool. Of course, you keep winning and you get to keep playing. Next thing you know, you got yourself a few bucks in dimes and you slip the fake ones in a back pocket." Trevor laughed, peered at his own gap-toothed grin in the rearview mirror.

The street tilted upwards through endless rows of old plaster adobe homes, wrought-iron cages bolted across their windows.

Remmie tugged at an earlobe and said, "You grew up around here?"

"Goddamn right. And happy as a pasta noodle, too."

The car crested the hill. Over the flat-roofed homes, Remmie saw the bay, a night-blackened tongue undulating beyond box-like warehouses and half-formed ship hulls. He cleared his throat. "We're taking him to the shipyard?"

"Used to be," Trevor said while ignoring him, "that a kid could grow up right around here. Make something of his goddamned self. Used to be, a kid could get himself a little shop, some kind of trade, a job in the yards, on a tuna boat. Used to be, donuts were good goddamn money. Like everything else in this world—used to be. Seems like that's all I say, fucking 'used to be.' Can you imagine making a living off goddamn donuts? What a hell of a country this used to be, huh?" Trevor shook his head like a wet dog and beads of sweat peppered Remmie's cheek.

Remmie wiped the sweat away with a grease-scarred

index finger. "Hell, where I grew up, I had a fine career gutting pigs. Now look at me."

"Now look at you," Trevor said.

"I could have had it easy."

"Sure could have. You had it made, neighbor." Trevor tapped the brakes as they reached the bottom of the hill, crossed through a four-way intersection without stopping, and cruised into an industrial area.

The headlights illuminated rust-flecked warehouses, beaten-down diesel rigs, and the slow dripping of outdated machinery abandoned in alleyways. Remmie saw a battered forklift tilted at an odd angle, a few empty, overturned dumpsters. "Doesn't look like much work to be had around here," he said. "Not now anyways."

"Used to be," Trevor said again. "Had ourselves some canneries down this way. Good money in it if you were a worker, I mean a real worker. Way it is now, all you find down here is scrap metal and—" He lifted his thumb at the trunk.

"Bodies," Remmie said.

"Body parts, neighbor." Trevor slowed, turned into an alleyway. The headlights splashed their whitewash along close walls etched with indiscernible graffiti. "The way to do it is to split the man up, like we did in the bathtub."

"You did." Remmie glanced at the fat man in the driver's seat, waited for his furrowed brow to smooth and broaden, for the killer to appear.

Trevor didn't seem to hear him. Instead, he accelerated toward the alleyway's fenced dead-end, stopped a few feet shy of the cut-through chain-link barrier. "Head and belly go here, and hands and feet go in a dumpster next to Reefer's Tune Up Station. Been doing it like this for a couple years now. Not so much as a sniff from the detectives uptown. Something about the current here, takes trash and sewage out to sea, lickety-split."

"And bodies," Remmie said. He unlatched his seatbelt.

"Body parts, neighbor. Make sure you get that. Body parts."

Remmie opened his door. He stood in the alleyway while the bay breeze slapped him in the face. The smell was an odd cocktail: Fish heads and factory waste, human sewage and gasoline spills. Beyond the chain-link, Remmie could see the bay tilting and listing in the darkness. He'd been in the city for a few weeks, but he'd never been down to see the bay, not to a point where he could smell it and hear the saltwater smacking against itself.

Trevor popped the trunk, grunted as he hefted a bag and dragged it around the car. The strained plastic made a sandpaper sound over the glass-strewn concrete. "Come on over and help me toss this sucker, neighbor. Time is a-wasting-away and we still got another delivery before breakfast."

Remmie smirked at the fat man and his heavy bag of pimp brains and belly. He said, "Do you think she loved him?" His chin dipped slightly. Remmie was talking about the dead pimp. "I mean, the kind of love people talk about?"

"Who's that?" Trevor adjusted his tie, drew the loosening knot tight to his throat. "You mean that girl, Veranda? The bitch who stole my Charger?"

Remmie nodded.

"Not a chance in merry hell, neighbor. They were colleagues is all, like you and me." Trevor tasted the air and signaled an important thought with a raised finger. "You know what, neighbor? I kind of like you. You're a sensitive son of a bitch, what with your penchant for silence and ruminating on love." Trevor squinted at Remmie, lowered his hand, and spit on the black Hefty bag. "But there's something about you." He traced Remmie's thin frame with both hands, like a man painting the air with both arms at once. "I need help finding this girl, Veranda. Especially if she went down to old Mexico. That's a rare-if-eyed air down there, and a man needs an accomplice."

"I got to work," Remmie said, "pay the rent."

"It's a job that pays."

Remmie shifted in his grease-splattered work boots. He looked down at his sweat-soaked Levis, gripped his thread-bare black t-shirt, felt the stiff curl of thrice-worn underwear chaffing his ass. A whole lot of good this fry cook gig was doing him. Remmie had little if anything to show for a few months of gut-gagging work. Burned fingers and an extra few pounds in his belly.

Free meals, sure.

Steady paycheck, sure.

Freedom and pleasure?

Not a goddamn chance—what did Trevor say?—in merry hell.

Remmie rolled his tongue across his jagged bottom teeth. He sighed and thought about it for a few moments. He could do with a road trip, with a bit of fun and mystery.

And Remmie could sure do with coming alive again.

He nodded slowly and said, "How much per day? And can I get some advance money?"

5

"**WHAT I LIKE IS A DECENT EGGS BENEDICT.** You ever order an eggs Benedict and get stuck with a set of hockey pucks?" Trevor leaned backwards in the booth and crossed his arms. When he shook his head, his fat cheeks shivered like raw chicken breasts. "You order a Benedict, and you expect a goddamn egg soft as silk. No exceptions. You expect clouds of yellow yolk on your tongue. You expect a piece of hot heaven in your fucking mouth. At least, I do." He lifted a steaming mug of coffee, dipped his tongue in it like an overheated pony, slammed it down on the table. "Sometimes, I think, what the fuck are we paying for here? I want to eat stale toast, I'll run down to Ralph's and get me a whole loaf. My uncle used to talk about quality goods, quality service. If you're selling something—I don't give two shits what it is—quality is all you've got. You're not selling donuts, burgers, diamond-fucking-rings. Hell, no. You're selling quality. People pay for quality."

Remmie stared out the diner's window at slow traffic along the street. It was five in the morning and the city was starting to awaken. A street cleaning machine lumbered along, its twirling brushes casting up mist and dust near the closest intersection. The street cleaning machine lumbered around the corner, out of view, and the stoplight turned red, green, yellow, red again. Remmie flexed the muscles in his right arm—he might have pulled something when he tossed the bag of arms and legs into the dumpster. You never think about how heavy a leg or arm is, not in your everyday life.

But Remmie knew: Arms and legs are heavy suckers.

Trevor kept up his chatter, didn't wait for Remmie to respond. "Quick thing about the waitress: That lady has been here at least six years. That's how long I've been coming here after my late nights at work. She gains about ten pounds a year, you believe that? Ten fucking pounds in butter and grease, and that's with all the walking she does."

The waitress was a tall, dark-haired woman with a take-no-shit glare. Yes, she was adorned with love handles, but Trevor himself was double the woman's size. Remmie upturned a corner of his mouth. "You don't have much room to talk, big man." It came out fast, before Remmie could stop himself. He didn't quite regret it, but he wondered if he should.

Trevor sipped from his coffee, swirled the hot liquid in his mouth, swallowed. He said, "What did you order again?"

"Pancakes, blueberry pancakes."

"You'll be as fat as me by the end of this meal." Trevor laughed. His belly shook against the table, rattled the soap-spotted silverware and coffee cups. "We'll be two fat asses on a road trip to Mexico—they better hide all the taco stands." He laughed again, placed a hand over his mouth. "Oh, jeez. I really like you, neighbor. You say what you mean, even if it's on accident."

23

Love Handles—the waitress—appeared at their booth and dropped the food. Remmie had a large stack already drenched in maple syrup. Trevor's eggs Benedict did not look promising. He poked at an egg with one finger, nodded.

"Feels like yellow heaven."

"Anything else for you, gentlemen?" That take-no-shit glare challenged Remmie and Trevor to ask for more of anything. It was a courtesy question.

"We're fine," Remmie said and watched Love Handles stomp back to the kitchen. He rolled his eyes at Trevor. "You better not tell her what you told me. That lady will kick some merry ass if you do."

Trevor leaned over his breakfast and looked Remmie square in the eye. "I just cut a pimp to pieces with a hacksaw. You think I give a shit about a plump waitress in a half-star diner down on Bum-stroll Avenue?"

Remmie sliced into his pancakes. "Maybe not, but she looks like she might hack us to pieces with a spoon." He shoved food into his mouth and talked through mashed up flour and butter. "What about this Veranda chick? And the fucking car you two were screaming about? You going to tell me the whole story? Or am I just along for the ride?" Remmie choked down another bite, grimaced. "This is like eating dirt. I should have ordered some fucking—"

"Eggs Benedict," Trevor said. "It's always good here." He ate with dainty knife strokes and a deft swirl of his fork. "See," he said, "I eat a French dish like I'm a Frenchman. Eloquent as a made-her-D. You and me," he thrust his fork tines at Remmie, "are going after one Miss Veranda B. Cline. Small town girl, but a rather skilled dancer and...Performance artist. I say that from firsthand experience. A number of firsthand experiences. Point is—"

"What's the 'B' stand for?"

Trevor lifted his eyebrows. "Ah, the 'B.' I made that bit up, to add some eloquence, you see. A little flourish of the mind. Literary license, if you will."

Remmie grunted.

"Veranda Cline comes to us from the fertile fields of Humboldt, C-A. Her parents though—rather unlike my boss's other girls—had some education. That's college, neighbor. Veranda got pissy with daddy, and she decided to extract profit from her body, a substantially profitable body, I might add."

"She was a looker." Remmie chewed harder, tried to crush his rubbery pancakes.

Trevor nodded. "That she was."

"Is?"

"And this," Trevor said, "is why I procured your services. Is, she is. And, if I'm thinking along the right lines, she very much is in my used-new Dodge Charger. And that's the very least of our problems because—"

"Why'd she take the car?" Remmie stopped chewing, stared at Trevor with a chin-solid expression. "Is there money in the car?"

Trevor's eggs Benedict was granted a reprieve from the ceaseless executions of his fork. He swallowed air a few times and said, "Yes, there was some money in the car."

"And what else?"

Trevor smiled. He licked his bottom lip and dipped his fork into a silky egg yolk, lifted it to his mouth and sucked on it. After he swallowed, he said, "There's a body in the trunk. A whole body—not...disassembled."

"But she didn't know about the—"

"No, she did not know about the body."

Remmie sighed. "Who is it? Some scumbag?"

"That depends on your definition of a scumbag. If you

call a cop a scumbag, yes—it's the body of a scumbag."

"A fucking cop?"

"A detective, actually. Homicide."

"Jee-zus," Remmie said. "Kee-rist."

"And the cop," Trevor said, "was kind of close with Veranda."

"How close?"

Trevor tilted his head from one shoulder to the other, stared down at his half-eaten eggs. He dropped his fork and breathed heavily at Remmie. "The cop was Veranda's older brother. He came down here to—"

"Get her out of the life."

"Buy her out, Actually."

Remmie said, "And you killed him."

Trevor nodded.

"And took his money?"

Trevor kept nodding.

Remmie stabbed a last triangular piece of pancake, slipped it into his mouth. He didn't say anything. There was nothing to say. He chewed and chewed and chewed.

After a long time, he swallowed.

6

VERANDA CLINE—THE WAY TREVOR SPENDS described her—was a short brunette with a nice ass, kind of made you think she could dance the Salsa. Her eyes were a bright green and she wore bangs over them, like a fifties starlet. The first time Trevor met her was at a Jazz club downtown; it was a small place, and everybody filed in one Friday to hear some L.A. guy play a few standards on piano. It was a free show, and Veranda was there. Trevor remembered she sat up front at a round table, an empty cocktail glass in front of her—she was alone.

With Trevor that night was his boss, a man named Leo Action; what Leo figured out in his mid-twenties was that he could work his way in on the city's vice crooks by running around like a tough cookie, shoving loaded guns in people's faces. All it took was balls and a pal to do the body work. The body work was Trevor's job. In fact, he and Leo had been working together for fifteen years, and they had a good thing going. Busy times, around the holidays and when big conventions came to town, they counted twenty Gs a week. Leo pushed in on street pimps, guys who thought they were running things, and made them pay him each week.

Hell, when you thought hard about all this, it wasn't even wrong, not in the way Father Larry down at St. Didacus talked about wrong.

Leo and Trevor—the way Trevor described it—were a kind of big city Robin Hood duo; they robbed the robbers, went crooked on the crooks, pimped the fucking pimps. And sometimes, like in the downtown Jazz club, they found a girl they could push into the life. An earner. It was Leo, Trevor said, who led them to Veranda's table. He sat down next to her and ordered a round of drinks for the three of them— Manhattans on the rocks, eighteen bucks a pop. With cherries on top. He introduced himself, introduced Trevor, and told Veranda she was the most beautiful girl he'd seen. That night, at least. A line like that got a laugh from Veranda; she appreciated humor. And, Trevor found out, she had a thing about honesty. Like, it drove her crazy when Leo wouldn't tell her who she was taking out on the weekends. Was it some Iowa-shit-town tire salesman with half a hard-on? Maybe a lowlife insurance executive from the other coast? Or, shit, was it a city councilman happy to have his wife out of town on sabbatical? Veranda needed to know what—and who—she was getting into.

But not Leo. No, Leo kept his own counsel, and that sometimes left Trevor, even his good buddy Trevor, in the goddamn dark. But the first night they met, Veranda laughed easy, threw back a quick trio of Manhattans, and left with the two of them before Mr. L.A. was done tickling the ivories. They ended up at Leo's place, a high-rise condominium on the city's east side. More drinks—at least three—and

Veranda was spouting off about how her dad, some university professor, wanted her to go to graduate school, how he wouldn't take no for an answer, and how—so she said—her parents were living some big chickenshit lie.

No lies here, Leo lied.

Nope, not that I've ever heard, Trevor lied.

But then again, Veranda never asked them what they did, who they were. And by the time she did ask, a week later, they didn't have to lie. She knew what they did because she was doing it for them. Funny thing about being a whore: You turn into one before you see it coming—it's like adolescence. And, hell, you can be a fancy, dressed up whore, but you're still what you are. The money was decent, a few hundred a week, and Leo got Veranda a small walkup, made her share it with one other girl. The guy she answered to, the sawed-up pimp who went by Donny, had a studio in Remmie's building. He also had a habit for roughing his girls up, something Leo didn't like. But both he and Trevor understood: Sometimes, it had to be done.

The beatings—this was according to Trevor—were what pushed Veranda to call her big brother. Turned out, the guy was a homicide dick in Sacramento. Nobody special. But he must have known what Veranda was caught between, that Leo—no matter what—would try to keep her. That's what the ten Gs were for, to buy Veranda out of the life, take her ass back to Humboldt C-A.

Thing was, Leo—Trevor said—didn't want to let Veranda run off to suburbia and college. He couldn't let it happen, he said, because she was the best he had; every day, she was the most beautiful girl he'd seen. That day, at least. But it was more than that, too. It was this homicide man trying to buy his sister away, trying to make it like Leo's life wasn't real, like Leo was a big fat nobody who never mattered. That's what got to him. And that's why he told Trevor what he did, to get the fucking money and make the cop disappear.

Trevor made it clear: It never was about Veranda; it was about some white kid with a smart mommy and daddy coming down to buy his little sister for a bag of chump change. It was class conflict. It was scumbags versus the law.

Lowlife versus easy street.

How did Leo Action put it?

It's us gutter rats against the good guys, Trevor.

That's what it was, how Leo put it.

According to Trevor, at least.

7

HERE REMMIE WAS, HIDING OUT in the Big City, and he felt like he was back home in the sticks—all the fucking stories were the same. You take a pretty girl and give her an attitude, put her hands and hips on the cold, gold stripper pole. What a sad story, right? And the dead detective. Hell, Remmie thought he might cry the guy a blue fucking river. From what Remmie knew, people died from dumb-shit disease every day. He'd been afflicted of the virus himself. Narrow escape, you know? What was the cop thinking? You don't try to negotiate with a strong man. Remmie—in all his inglorious anti-wisdom—knew that much. No, sir. You put a shotgun to the fucker's head and you pull the trigger or make him think you will. All this talk got Remmie thinking about an uncle he had, a slum-digger known as Frank Diamond.

Uncle Frank used to throw darts at red sparrows. He was a man who didn't mind a million futile attempts if he got one in the head. All it takes is one. When Remmie was about fourteen—give or take—uncle Frank took him on a trip to a gambling town on the Arizona-Nevada border. Place called Laughlin, right there on the Colorado River with about ten casinos jutting straight up like snapped toothpicks. Remmie stayed in the room while Frank went out for the evening. He passed the time watching cartoons on the motel room tv, buying cheap candy bars and potato chips from a vending machine down the hall.

It's about two in the morning when uncle Frank stumbles into the room. In fact, he's so far gone that Remmie has to open the door for him. Uncle Frank tripped over himself before he reached the bed, lay slumped on the thin carpet. But what Remmie noticed, what he couldn't not notice, were the red stains on his uncle's hands. Remmie wiped the man's fingers with a tissue, and all that red came away like…Well, like blood. He slapped uncle Frank and said, "Where the fuck you been, old man?" Remmie leaned him into the bed, tried to prop his head up against the mattress. "Wake the fuck up, dammit."

"What you want?" Frank's Kmart suit—not even close to tailored—was rumpled tight across his shoulders.

"Where you been?"

"I been killing her," Frank said.

Remmie figured he was using a figure of speech. "Killing what?"

"The girl."

"What girl?"

"The whore. The whore from the Edgewater."

The Edgewater was a hotel a few blocks up the strip. Remmie went into the bathroom and filled a glass with tap water. He returned and dumped the glass over his uncle's head. "It's time to get up, old man. You're not talking any fucking sense. Where the hell you been?"

"Killing the whore, dammit. I been killing the whore." Frank tasted the insides of his mouth, choked on his own saliva.

"What do you mean, 'killing the whore?'"

Frank raised a hand, held up one finger slick with near-dried blood. He put the finger into his mouth, slurped.

Remmie almost threw up, put both hands over his mouth to stop it. He didn't know what to do: Was the old man playing with him? Was he confused? Where in the hell did all the blood come from? This is all a joke, Remmie thought, it has to be a joke.

But as he watched Frank pass out and slump to the carpet, Remmie's stomach dropped—this was real.

A few minutes later, in the motel's parking garage, it didn't take Remmie long to find his uncle's crooked-bodied Ford Ranger; it was emerald green with a black front fender and a cracked rear window. It did, however, take Remmie a long time to open the passenger side door. Through the slit in the cracked window, he traced a vaguely feminine form. The shape unsettled him. Remmie didn't like how one of the legs—slim, finely-formed—jutted against the steering wheel. It wasn't natural. He was reminded of his uncle's odd gesture, his fat lips slurping at a bloody finger.

And when Remmie did get up enough nerve to unlock the Ford and open the door, he was shocked. But not surprised.

It was the first dead body Remmie ever saw. She was small, too small to believe, and Remmie thought she was beautiful. Tight blonde curls and half-open blue eyes. A pert nose with an upturned tip. Gray-blue halter top with fake jewels lowered across her chest. Swaths of moon-colored eye shadow.

And, like with the pimp, a sticky and undeniable red-black tint of blood.

A neck wound, Remmie saw.

A slit throat.

Another small-town story unwinding like a made-for-shit tv movie plot. That was the first body Remmie ever made disappear, but he wouldn't tell that to Trevor. No, sir. He'd keep that one to himself. Sometimes, when he woke up in the middle of the night, Remmie thought about uncle Frank. He wondered: What in the hell is that man up to these days?

8

BACK IN THE MUSTANG, with a bacon-grease scent chewing at Remmie's nerves, Trevor Spends used his cell phone to call Leo Action. The morning was gray and damp, stoplights—void of traffic—flashing from one color to the other; Remmie stared at the wet streets while Trevor talked to his boss.

"Leo, I got some good news, and I got some bad." A short pause and Trevor grunted. "Look now, Leo. I told you, I said it wouldn't be cake to find the girl—we both know: She's a smart little sister." Trevor scratched his neck, pushed his slick hair into the Mustang's headrest. "The bad is… Shit, I shot the pimp."

A vomit-like barrage of shouting came over the phone line. Remmie turned to watch as Trevor clenched his jaw, tried to interject. The man had to endure thirty seconds of Leo's curses. Remmie shook his head, went back to staring out the window, but then decided to rest his eyes.

"It was a goddamn accident, Leo," Trevor said. "I got rid

of it...him." A pause. "It's taken care of, Leo. That's what took me so long to call. But there's good news, too. Matter of fact, it's sitting right next to me." More shouting. Trevor said, "No, it's not Veranda. It's a guy I ran into—he's going with me down to Mexico, help me find the girl. We're going to get all this taken—"

Remmie winced as Leo's shouting poured forth from the tiny phone. He sounded like a mangy cross between a drill sergeant and an elephant seal.

Trevor punched the steering wheel and said, "I told you we're going to get the money back. You know we're going to get it. Don't I always get the money? Haven't I always pulled in the paper for you? Haven't I, goddammit? I said I'd find Veranda, and I will. I said I'd kill the cop, and I did. And now, I'm saying I'll get the fucking money and—Yes, I'll get the Dodge back." He hissed with impatience. "That goes without saying. Jesus, I love that fucking car. You know I love it, Leo. When did you get so sensitive about this kind of thing? You know we run into this stuff sometimes. It goes with the—"

Remmie opened his eyes, stared at an old woman—bent-backed and decrepit—pushing a mud-coated shopping cart across the street. She shuffled forward without checking for traffic.

Trevor sighed, grunted a few affirmations. "I been down to Mexico plenty of times, Leo. We'll stay out of the stripper joints. Yes, of course. No strippers, Leo. I get it. This is all business—there's some good money in that fucking car, and I want it back as much as you do. I promise you—no fucking strippers. And, yes, I'll keep the drinking to a minimum." More grunts. A few low hums from Trevor's throat. He nodded once, and clicked the cell phone off, tossed it onto the dashboard. "Fucking hell," Trevor said. "The man won't forgive a mistake if you pay him for it. Make a good wife for somebody."

"Maybe you just aren't paying enough," Remmie said.

"Trust me, I get that money back, it's plenty."

Remmie buckled his seatbelt, settled into his bucket seat. "I guess this means we're going for some international travel, huh?"

Trevor started the Mustang, tapped the throttle. Behind them, an exhaust mist shot from the mufflers, drifted into the damp air. "Crossing borders," Trevor said, "that there is—most definitely and always—something we are about to do. And us two, good neighbor, are going to do a damn good job of it…"

● ● ●

After crossing the Mexican-American border in San Ysidro, the first place Remmie and Trevor stopped was a strip club called El Gato Negro. So much for promises to the boss man, Remmie thought. And so much for a man's last shred of decency. It was a smelly place—cooked lard and sweat— with a skinny man at the front door. He waved them in with a smile and said, "Buenos Días, mis amigos. Welcome to the gato den." Remmie and Trevor took seats at a round table beside the main stage, watched a girl with short black hair dance out of tempo to a Madonna song. A waitress appeared before them and asked for their drink order.

Remmie noticed the waitress was underage, fourteen at the most, a precocious looking girl with thick eyebrows. "Tecaté," he said. "No limón para mi." He smiled at his own accent. High school Spanish—it did a man good.

"Let's see, miss," Trevor said. "I'll take a margarita on the rocks. You can hold the salt, but let's add an extra shot of the rough stuff."

The waitress sprinted to the bar, started to make the

margarita herself. This early in the morning, the strip club was near empty, cleared out after a long night of creepy American patronage. Remmie saw two clean-cut white kids sleeping at a corner table, both their heads slumped against sticky forearms. "You think they had a nice night? Didn't even make it back home."

Trevor stood and stomped across the club, took a side-long glance at the dancer, but pulled out a chair next to the sleeping Americans. He sat down with a long, sweeping heave of breath.

From across the club, Remmie watched with curiosity.

Trevor slapped the table with both hands and the two kids yanked their faces from their arms. Both had red cheeks and sleep-crusted eyes. One kid rubbed his forehead and said, "Who the fuck are you?"

"I'm the man asking the fucking questions," Trevor said. He dipped a hand into his suit coat, pulled out his cell phone. He found a picture on the phone and slid it across the table, leaned forward in the chair until it creaked.

The dancer on stage mooned Remmie. She half-smiled when Madonna gave way to a slinky Guns & Roses number. Remmie shuddered at the raucous drums and guitar. He tried to hear what the two clean-cut kids said to Trevor, but the music drowned them out. A minute later, Trevor was back at the table. He smiled at the waitress when she brought the drinks, handed her a crisp twenty-dollar bill. Again, he set the cell phone on the table, pointed at Veranda's picture. Remmie, too, leaned forward to examine the girl for whom he was searching. Something happened to Remmie when he saw Veranda's face for the first time; it was a thing he had trouble describing, like a hand clenching and then giving way inside him. The closest thing he'd ever felt to it was watching his first son's birth. It was a feeling that opened him up, gassed his heart with heat.

In the image, Veranda wore little makeup; her hair was tied up in a ponytail, jutted out behind her left ear. Her eyes—emerald green—looked through the image beneath her straight bangs, like she was seeing into Remmie. He cleared his throat, tried to pull his eyes from the phone, but the nose...Veranda's nose, slightly upturned and, yes, pert, reminded him of the girl who his uncle Frank...Oh, his uncle Frank—enough of that. Veranda was beautiful, and she made Remmie—he didn't know how—burn up inside. He felt feverish there at the table, lifted the Tecaté to his forehead, pressed it there like a branding iron. The waitress shook her head, tried to make change for Trevor. He placed a hand on hers and smirked.

"Gracías, mister," she said.

Trevor watched her vanish into the dark before turning back to the stage. The dancer was swinging her hips at them, staring at Trevor with near-dead eyes, purple lipstick clinging to lopsided lips. "Let's take a look at this, neighbor," he said. "Let's go ahead and watch ourselves the show."

Remmie didn't respond to Trevor, and he didn't stare at the mechanical movements of the stripper. No, he sat there with a cold beer can pressed to his head, his eyes unblinking, irises focused like gunsights on the digital image of Veranda Cline.

Remmie couldn't look away. He was hypnotized.

9

THE CLOSEST REMMIE EVER GOT to Mexico—before he met Trevor—was a job heating flour tortillas at a place called Tio's back in his hometown. Remmie didn't last long in that job. Turned out he was a much better French fry man than he was a tortilla flipper. Still, he loved the food, and he always did like to look at Mexican women. Was Tijuana what he imagined? The truth was that Remmie wasn't sure what he imagined, not anymore.

After three hours of watching strippers and drinking cheap beer, standing outside El Gato Negro, Remmie stared at the traffic on the avenida. Most surprising to him was the fact that—contrary to newspaper clippings—Mexicans drove lots of new cars. Sure, they had some different models here, or similar models with different names, but everybody had a shiny two-door with a little four-banger beneath the hood.

Both he and Trevor leaned against the Mustang's rear

bumper and smoked cigarettes. Remmie didn't often smoke, but something about being in Mexico made him want to have one. Call it tossing caution to the wind. Trevor, with Remmie in tow, had already asked the shopkeepers along this side of the street whether they'd seen a new Dodge Charger in the last day or so; they came up empty in each place. 'No, señor—nada,' they all said.

Nada. Nada. Nada.

On the street, a twenty-something with dreadlocks zoomed past on a knockoff Vespa. "Man," Remmie said, "It's like being in San Diego, except Mexican-ish. If I knew it was so hip, I'd have been down here more often."

Trevor sighed, dangled the cigarette between his lips. "This here is the tourist zone, amigo. They keeps it all nice and pretty. Believe me, it ain't all perfect. We gonna find the dark side soon enough."

"What made you come here first?" Remmie motioned at the strip club's nondescript gray door, still guarded by the skinny Mexican.

"Oh, I know this area. I just thought to ask around is all." Trevor grunted and straightened his bulky frame beside the Mustang. His once immaculate suit was wrinkled after their morning strip club siesta. "What I think we might do is run back to the border, see the places where Veranda might have asked for directions when she crossed. Now that I think about it, might be she just kept on the highway, took it down to Rosarito Beach or even Ensenada."

Remmie wasn't surprised. "Why stay here, right? I mean, if you're trying to get away and all, you put as many miles as you can between you and…"

"Your pimp?" Trevor looked at Remmie, stared at him with cool contemplation. "That what you wanted to say?"

"I was going to say, your sugar daddy."

"Ain't nothing sugar about Leo Action," Trevor said. "You can rest assured of that. If it paid, the man would put salt on his fucking ice cream."

"Why are you still running around for him, if he's so bad for souls?"

Trevor thought about it. "I guess it goes back to us growing up together. You have anybody like that, a person you can't get away from?"

"Not like that, no." He thought about home. Not much there to remember except abandoned train tracks, a few mobile home parks, some half-ass restaurants, most of which he'd been fired from—Remmie considered himself a journeyman cook. "I guess I understand though," he said. "Loyalty, that's what you're saying."

Trevor shook his head. "I'm saying, obligation. Loyalty—that's an option. But an obligation? I mean, it's something you have to do. No ifs, ands, or fucking buts. Like we did last night, you know?"

"Kill the pimp?"

"Not the killing," Trevor said. "That was an accident. I'm talking about the other stuff, how we had to—"

"Get rid of him."

"Make him disappear." Trevor clapped once, let the cigarette drop from his mouth onto the sidewalk. He placed his hands on his hips. "Well, amigo," he said. "Me thinks we need to ask around some more, get us a lead on the pretty girl and the shiny car. I know a taco shop for lunch—you will dig it." He shuffled to the driver's side door, opened it. "Let's go, amigo. On the lay, baby. On. The. Lay. When in Rome..."

Tacos sounded tasty to Remmie. But the other stuff, this 'what we had to do' talk, made him nervous. For the first time, Remmie thought about what Trevor meant to do to Veranda Cline, what he might be obligated to do. The image from

Trevor's cell phone was stuck in Remmie's head. It flashed through him like a projection. Did she know her brother was dead? Did she know that she was the one—on accident, but still—who got the man killed, that she was driving around with her dead brother in her trunk?

And, beyond all that, did she know Trevor was chasing her?

10

"YOU WANT THIS FOR YOUR GIRL, AMIGO?" The flower vendor, a tough looking kid with a jagged scar on his chin, tried to hand Remmie a red rose wrapped in clear cellophane. "Take it and make your lady happy, cabrón."

Remmie was hustling to keep up with Trevor along a street just beyond the border crossing. They passed a row of dusty white taxis, their antsy drivers waving people over, trying to steal an extra dollar for a cheap run to the shopping district. Vendors milled among the morning influx of American tourists. The thousands of people who crossed the border on foot each day spilled onto the street, a dirty lane peopled with taxi drivers, empanada salesman, beggars, and the occasional wily huckster—nothing like a border crossing to bring out a town's best and worst hustlers. Ahead, Remmie watched Trevor wave to a squat taxi driver eating tacos off the hood of his car. Trevor was saying, "Ramón, what up my brother? It's been a couple months…"

The flower salesman tried again to shove the rose into Remmie's hands. "Only three bucks, amigo. This rose last your lady a week, maybe longer. Bring it to your girl on the other side." The kid shrugged. "Or maybe bring it to your Mexican lady, huh?"

Remmie pushed the rose away, tried to shake the kid, but they walked in step, crossed the street like two characters in a buddy sitcom. "Man, kid," Remmie said, "I'm not going to buy a rose from you. I don't have a girl."

"No girl? What? You lie, amigo."

They reached the other side of the street, moved beneath an awning where rows of patched-together vans waited, the pickup spot for locals, people too poor—or cheap—to pay a taxi fare. Remmie stopped and looked the kid in the face. "I'm the wrong man for a rose, buddy. I got no girl. Not right now, I don't."

"Man, you give this rose to whoever you want. It's for that special—"

"No rose, pal," Remmie said. He was watching Trevor place a hand on the squat driver's shoulder, start to squeeze. The guy squeezed his taco—meat, salsa, and chopped onions toppled out onto the pavement. Remmie thought he might need to rein Trevor in, rely on dialog, not instant violence. But the kid was in his face with this fucking rose. "I thought I told you—"

"Take it to that girl you're looking for, amigo. The one with the nice ride and all the money, huh?"

Remmie stopped, met the kid's dark wet eyes.

"I know you want to find that girl, amigo." The kid nodded at the row of taxis parked across the street. "Heard your fat jefe asking about her."

"What did you hear?"

"You're looking for a pretty lady in a white Dodge. A

Charger. Nice car, amigo. That's a nice ride. I saw her here the other day, stopped to ask—"

"You saw Veranda here?"

The kid turned, pointed the rose at a half-filled parking area, a pay lot for the nearby food court. "She's right over there two days ago, talking on a cell phone. I seen her crying over there, screaming at somebody."

Remmie looked past the kid, saw Trevor haul back a big fist, hammer it against the squat man's cheek. The man's legs buckled, but Trevor held him up by his shirt, pressed him against the taxi's front bumper. Remmie started to shout, "Trevor! Over here—"

But the kid pressed closer to him. He smelled like drug-store cologne and cornmeal. "She's scared, amigo. Your girl is scared. I could see it, a look in her eyes. Like she can't get away from the fear, amigo."

"What do you know about it, kid? You're just a flower boy."

"I see everything, amigo. I work here every day, all fucking day. Six years now, amigo. But all that time, I never seen a girl scared like yours."

"She's not my girl," Remmie said. Trevor punched the taxi driver again, let him sink to his knees. Trevor lifted the paper tray of tacos, dumped it over the man's head. Remmie sighed. "I don't even know her, only seen her picture."

"But you already love her, amigo. I can see it."

Remmie shook his head, annoyed. "You know where she went, or is this you hustling me?" He tried to push past the kid, but they faced each other belly to belly. "You don't know shit, otherwise you'd tell me."

"Twenty dollars," the kid said, "I give you the rose for the girl."

"You said three bucks."

"This rose has a special message, amigo."

Remmie looked the kid up and down: worn-through jeans, a wrinkled collared shirt, fresh shave over the white-edged scar on his chin. Remmie slid a twenty-dollar bill from his wallet, folded it in half. "You better have something real, kid. I don't like to pay for shit I already know, like she's fucking scared."

The kid took the twenty, handed the rose to Remmie. He lifted his chin and said, "She's going down to Puerto Santo Tomás, amigo. I heard her say it on the phone, talking to some guy from San Diego. Right after that, she left."

"You're sure? Puerto…"

"Santo Tomás, amigo. Little fishing village."

"If you're fucking with me, I'm going—"

"I promise, cabrón. And the rose is yours to keep." The kid jogged back across the street, vanished in the mass of tourists and border hustlers.

When Remmie reached Trevor, the taxi driver was gasping for air, breathing through fat bloody lips and a crooked tooth or two. He tried to lift his head but couldn't. Trevor was breathing hard too, his chest lifting and shuddering above his big belly. "Fucker won't give me anything, neighbor. This son of a bitch is acting like he—"

"I've got a gift for you, Trevor."

"The fuck is this?"

Remmie handed Trevor the cellophane-wrapped rose. He leaned casually against the taxi, stared at the hard-breathing man sprawled on the pavement. He felt Trevor's big inquisitive eyes on him.

"You're out shopping for flowers? I'm trying to get information. You're out here buying flowers and playing tourist. Fuck me," Trevor said. "I promised you good money for this job. But that means you got to—"

"Puerto Santo Tomás," Remmie said and crossed his arms.

Trevor looked down at the taxi driver, reared back a foot and kicked the man in the ribs. He huffed a painful breath and groaned. "Puerto Santo Tomás, huh?" He sniffed the rose.

"It's a fishing village."

"I know what the fuck it is," Trevor said. He stared for a moment at the taxi driver, looked back over his shoulder at the crowd of tourists. Trevor lifted the rose again, sniffed hard and grimaced at the aroma.

11

WHILE TREVOR POWERED THE MUSTANG through traffic on the four-lane highway, Remmie watched Tijuana neighborhoods unspool outside the driver's side window. Lots of tin roofs and oddly angled brick walls built into each other. The occasional chicken coop and, as they neared the coast, more stucco-built structures, condominiums done mission style. He said, "I bet you can live down here pretty cheap, survive on tacos and Tecaté."

"Maybe," Trevor said. He glared at a bent-bodied Chevy pickup truck, accelerated past the mustached driver. "But you buy a bag of coke from the wrong gaucho and you end up with a dismounted head, your torso dangling from a light pole. It's a bad city for the criminal-type."

Remmie shook his head. "I figure all that's a myth, this thing about the cartels slicing everybody up. We don't even hear about it in the California papers." Up ahead, he saw the tall brim of a concrete arena rising above the road. "What's that over there?"

"Bull fighting ring."

"They still do that here?"

"Thank the lord, they do." Trevor said. "The reason no newspaper types write about Tijuana is because they'll end up in a shallow ditch. It's like writing your own obituary. At least for an American it is."

"You sound so worldly when you speak of the Mexican people. How do you know so much about the place? I thought you were San Diego muscle."

Trevor shrugged, checked the mirrors before switching lanes. "Leo sends me down here sometimes to drop off packages. Believe me, I make my regular stops, but then I'm back across the border."

"You bringing money down?"

"Enough to kill a pack mule."

"Well, look at it this way: Veranda Cline already did your job for you." Remmie found himself needling Trevor, trying to find a way to hit the man where it might hurt. If he had such a place. The Mustang rounded a curve in the road, throttled down and settled onto the highway running parallel to the coast. Looking out his own window now, Remmie saw the blue ocean peek from beyond rooftops with black water tanks perched atop them.

Trevor didn't respond to Remmie's mention of Veranda, but instead said, "I was you, I wouldn't think too hard about Tijuana. You live in San Diego and you're white. TJ might as well be Hong Kong. Don't overexert that little brain of yours. Tell me again, what did the flower boy say?"

"He said he heard the girl—Veranda—talking on the phone to some dude in San Diego, saying that she was headed to the fishing village."

"He say a name? Who it was on the phone with her?"

"No, he didn't."

"You ask?"

Remmie breathed hard through his nose. "I didn't know I should, didn't think about it. I'm sorry. It happened fast; the kid was there, and then, shit, he was gone."

"Yeah, those street vendors live one Mexican minute at a time. That happens to you again, grab the guy by the neck and slam him into something. Anything, a brick wall, a fire engine, a shitty taco stand. You do that and you'll save yourself twenty bucks."

"I'm sure the kid can use the money."

"What are you," Trevor said, "UNICEF?"

Remmie found himself irritated; he realized, for the first time that morning, he hadn't slept. First, it was the pimp's... disposal. Then it was breakfast and the border crossing. After that, the strip club and the twenty-dollar clue along with the rose, now sitting on the backseat, still wrapped in its cellophane. He shook off the comment, knew Trevor was playing with him. If only to pass the time. "We going to sleep anytime soon? That's how this whole thing started. You and your pal the pimp were keeping me up, remember?" Remmie felt the exhaustion in his joints, an ache that stretched into his muscles. His feet hurt, too. Like they always did when he got off work.

Trevor nodded, pressed out his upper lip with the tip of his tongue. "I remember alright, neighbor. Tell you what: You can sleep on the drive down the coast. But first, we're going to get ourselves some perrónes."

"What's that?"

"Tacos, neighbor. Means, awesome-rad-cool-delicious. One-of-a-kind here." Trevor slowed the Mustang, hit a wraparound exit which pointed the car northward along a two-lane frontage road. The ocean swung to the driver's side window, flat and blue as midnight ice. They cruised along, rolled through a stop sign. The road made a gradual transformation to avenida, lots of shops and art galleries springing from the pavement along wide sidewalks. "Best tacos in the big old world," Trevor said, "right here in Rosarito Beach."

Remmie's stomach still felt full. He tasted the sweet fluffiness of his earlier plate of pancakes. He looked from the road down to Trevor's belly; the soft lump beneath his coat rubbed against the Mustang's steering wheel. "You think we need to eat this soon? We had breakfast, like, a few hours ago."

"That was just a mid-morning snack," Trevor laughed. "This'll be breakfast. A few perrónes and a beer is all we're doing. After that, you can sleep. I promise. Cross my heart and hope you die."

● ● ●

Already a line at the open-air taco joint and Remmie stared at pretty tourist girls with short-shorts and bikini tops, found himself salivating at the smell of marinated meat and roasted green peppers. He and Trevor moved steadily forward in the line, watched traffic crawl past the outdoor shop with its hot-shit line cooks in Ray-Bans and too-tight black polo shirts. The big thing was that the main line cook, a guy with a lopsided smile and beer belly, used dual cleavers to chop the meat on top of a cut tree trunk. Part of the show, Remmie guessed. But there were a lot of people here for the food. That meant, to Remmie, these soldiers were doing something right. Hell, where Remmie worked, they prayed for regular customers, and his place was good. This joint, all the way down here in little old Mexico, was killing it.

Trevor said, "First time I came down here I was looking for a guy named Redondo, L.A. type from up north, thought he was hot shit with the ladies. Decided not to pay for a, you know, service he procured."

"Split on one of Leo's girls, huh?"

"That's right. And Leo's thing, you pay for what you order, even if you don't take it. So, this guy, this Redondo, he rents a car and runs down here, stays at the Rosarito Beach Hotel, just a few blocks south. Guy acts like he's tough, flashes cash everywhere, tips well. I'm watching him in the bar one night and he's tipping the bartender like crazy, buying people drinks. I'm thinking, 'He's got so much cash, why not pay Leo's girl?' I'm wondering what his deal is."

"So?" They moved forward a couple steps in line. One of the line cooks shouted at a passing car. The driver honked twice, revved the engine.

Trevor rubbed sweat from the back of his neck, fiddled with his knotted tie.

"Why don't you wear something more comfortable?"

Trevor wagged his finger. "Oh, no. Leo wants us to look professional at all times, like we know what we're doing."

Remmie thought about his blue jeans and t-shirt. "What about me?"

"We'll get you a Hawaiian shirt down in Ensenada, stop off in one of those waterfront shops. Maybe a cheap fedora too. For show."

Remmie laughed. Something funny about this whole situation, like his previous life was a picture he painted in a dream, and this was his real life, except this one seemed more like a myth or—what did they call those?—a fairy tale. "Me in a fedora, that's not the best kind of show."

"Hey," Trevor said, "a fedora makes a man seem grown up, like he's halfway smart or something. Like he's made."

"That's all it takes?"

"We need to get you a pistol, too. Something untraceable."

"Jesus. I don't need a pistol for—"

"Never know what can happen down here, neighbor."

Remmie noticed a few people in line look back at them. He shrugged and said, "That's funny, Trevor. Enough with the joking."

Trevor said, "Like I was saying, with this son of a bitch Redondo: He's flashing cash like he's a trust fund kid, buying people drinks, taking dinner bills for people. Odd, right? Well, when I go up to his room to wait—I got a hook-up with the cleaning staff—I look around and, sure as shit, he's got a lot of money. One suitcase full of cash, like he's cleaned out a bank account, come down here to blow it all."

"And?"

"He comes back to the room and, you know, I'm there, drinking tequila and waiting. Man is not surprised at all; it's like I'm a friend of his, just there having a drink. We sit across from each other at this little table on the balcony, listen to the waves crashing on the beach, the breeze coming through the palm trees. Sitting across from me, the guy is steel. I say, 'You know me?' He says, 'You're the machine Leo sent, the guy who's gonna kill me.' I ask him what makes him think I'm going to kill him. The man starts laughing. Can you picture it? He's going on laughing and I find this urge in myself; I reach across the table and grab his bottom lip, yank his face down against the table. And then he's crying and laughing at the same time, like a kid does, if you've ever seen it."

Remmie noticed more people turning to look at them.

Trevor kept his story moving: "I bang him around a bit and it comes out this guy's wife left him. Sob story, okay? The worst kind, too. They had two kids, daughters, teen girls, and the wife got it on with another guy, fell in love with him. Turns out, this cat, acting all brave and laughing in my face, can't face the fact his wife loves some other man. He can't deal with the whole thing; he isn't man enough, you see."

Remmie wanted this to hurry and finish. "Okay, so what happened?"

"What comes out is he ripped Leo off because he knew— our girl told him—that Leo would make him pay. Money, flesh, whatever it took."

"I don't understand." Now people turned away, tried to act like they weren't listening. The line proceeded. Remmie cracked his knuckles. They were third in line, about to order, but he felt like they were walking the plank.

"Man wanted to commit suicide, but he was too afraid. To do it himself, you see? He's sitting there at the table laughing, and I'm thinking he's making fun of me, jawing me. But that's not it—fucker went crazy. He wanted me—" Trevor whispered the last bit—"to kill him. You believe that? The man ripped off Leo just so he could run off and have the muscle chase him down. He ripped Leo off to get himself buried."

Remmie gulped. "What did you do?"

Trevor chuckled, yanked at his belt. "I obliged the man," he said. "I obliged him his wish. Way I see it, you got to keep a balance in this life. You need your bodies, and you need your gravediggers. I got used to the idea, neighbor…I'm one of the diggers. Anyhow, after that I came over here and had me some—"

It was their turn. Remmie and Trevor stepped forward, smiled at the line cooks and their magic act, tacos appearing like phantoms.

Trevor said, "Tres para me, amigo. And for my friend here, too."

"Si," Remmie said, "tres para me."

12

REMMIE DID FALL ASLEEP on the forty-minute drive down the coast, caught himself nodding off to the slow hum of the Mustang's tires. He dreamed about burying the girl Frank Diamond killed. Not too far outside Laughlin, headed west if he remembered right, Remmie found an old dirt road leading to a silver mine—he recalled the name: Split Quartz Road.

Imagine this fourteen-year-old kid shifting through a Ford Ranger's cranky gear box, a dead stripper tucked into the passenger seat. He even buckled her seatbelt. And the whole time, all the way out of town and into the desert, Remmie held back the vomit taste pushing up his throat and into his mouth. He left his uncle Frank passed out in the hotel room, stole the man's keys. Remmie popped the clutch a few times at red lights on the main avenue, kept checking his mirrors for cops. Somehow, with that acid taste spreading through his whole body, Remmie put the Ford into a straight ten-mile gallop and found the dirt road, turned off in a cloud of dust. He noticed the stripper's head bouncing like a doll's while he burned through curves and punched the gas. Remmie didn't go too far before he stopped the Ford and dragged the girl from the cab.

Dig a grave? No time for that. No patience for that. He was fourteen, about as close to a kid as he'd ever be again, and he was trying to make his uncle's bad business disappear. What Remmie did was topple the girl's body into a dry creek bed, shove dirt and creosote branches over her, try to make it so only the coyotes would know she was there. Hell, Remmie knew her body would be gone in a week, food for the vultures. No need to bury flesh and bone in the heat of the desert, not when you knew the world would have its way.

But this wasn't the real thing. It wasn't what really happened—nope, it was a dream.

And in the dream, Remmie didn't see the dead girl's face. He saw Veranda Cline's face. That similar upturned and pert nose, but deep green eyes with knowing irises.

That's what woke him up with a sharp gasp.

Trevor slapped Remmie's chest with back of his hand. "The good thing is you don't snore. The best partners don't snore. You got that part down, I'll give you that."

"I say anything?"

"Something about sticky first gear, but I couldn't catch it. Sounded like mumbo-jumbo to me. You casting some kind of spell in your nightmares?"

Out the windshield, Remmie saw the loose makings of a port city ahead: the ramshackle assortment of resort buildings and adobe-style shops, a blue shade of Pacific Ocean to the west, bobbing fishing trawlers passing each other on the sea. "That the fishing village?"

Trevor shook his head and said, "That's Ensenada, neighbor. Cute little spot, popular with the touristas. Puerto Santo

Tomás is another two hours down the coast, give or take. You've only been passed out for a little while—we got to stop here though, get you a new uniform."

Remmie sighed. "We going to eat again?"

Trevor laughed that fat belly laugh. "Ah, there you go again. I could do with a fish taco, but maybe for dinner, or an afternoon snack. Thing about Ensenada is they got a whole troop of nosy cops. Guys trying to make their names on drug busts. We're in and out, just need a tourist shop."

Remmie pried at the collar of his black t-shirt, felt how stiff it was, full of grease and kitchen heat. "I guess I could do with a new shirt."

"Get you a hat too," Trevor said. "And I happen to know a guy might sell us a pistol."

"Like I said, I don't need—"

"I say you need one," Trevor said, "you need one."

Remmie leaned forward in his seat, squinted at flashing lights up ahead of them on the highway. "What the hell is this? Looks like it's before the toll booth."

About three hundred yards from them was a large toll booth. It was easy to make out with its white trim, shady overhang, and dinky booths. But before the booth, parked along the highway, was a long line of beige-colored military trucks, their toothy tires biting into the road's shoulder. In front of a line of slowing cars, Remmie spotted two Mexican guys in military fatigues—teenagers it looked like—holding automatic rifles and asking questions of drivers and passengers. In the trucks, Mexican soldiers waited patiently, bored young men in ski masks and the same fatigues.

"Checkpoint," Trevor said. "Mexican Marines, neighbor. They're probably looking for some drugs, a mule heading down the peninsula."

"You got a gun, don't you?"

Trevor nodded. "That I do, but don't you worry."

"Don't worry? Jesus-fuck, Trevor. These guys look like they're—"

"You let me handle it, neighbor. I got a couple teenagers of my own. Don't think I can't handle some Mexicans with pimples. They're just kids is all."

"With automatic weapons." Remmie's heart beat fast, pounded against his breastbone.

Smirking, with a gleam in his eyes, Trevor said, "They couldn't fire those weapons if I had a set of pliers clinched on their greasy balls."

This fucking guy, Remmie thought. If anything, he was confident. Maybe, Remmie kept thinking, that confidence is the final bullet in my head. Still, he'd never been down to Me-hi-co; maybe, like Trevor said, he ought to let the veteran handle this. And if he got put in a Mexican prison? Well, so be it. Was it any worse than frying potatoes and burning beef?

And all that for peanuts?

Probably, Remmie thought, but not by much.

● ● ●

"¿A dónde vamos?" The Marine peered in through the driver's side window, glared at Remmie with disinterested eyes. On the passenger side, the other Marine, this one a taller kid with a baby face, held his rifle across his chest, watched the line of cars following them.

Trevor cleared his throat. "A Ensenada," he said. "Get us a good time." Trevor's teeth flashed between his flappy cheeks. "Me and my pal are going for some drinks and lobster, seenyour. You want to come on down with us?"

The Marine didn't return the smile or, from what Remmie could tell, register the joke. "For what?" He said it in thick-tongued English. "Ensenada for what?"

"Like I said," Trevor cleared his throat again. "We want us some drinks and women. Damas, seen-your. Más damas."

The Marine nodded. He motioned at the back of the car. "Let me see in this trunk."

Remmie thought: Holy shit—they really are looking for something. He saw the image of black hefty bags in his head. About five hours previous, a dead pimp was chopped up in that trunk. It was empty now, but if they were searching the trunk, would they search the car?

Trevor popped the trunk, dug a hand into his breast pocket while the Marine ambled to the car's rear. The second Marine, on Remmie's side, watched them with a flat expression. Trevor came out with a roll of twenties, unfolded it and peeled five bills out, rested them flat on the dashboard above the steering wheel.

Remmie said, "The fuck are you doing?"

"Keeping our options open, neighbor."

"That's a fucking bribe—"

Trevor pressed a finger to his lips. "Quiet, neighbor. We got to keep our options open. You go ahead and trust me on this one."

The trunk slammed, and the Marine reappeared at the window. "Search inside," he said motioning at the back seat.

"Oh, why's that, seen-your? It's just the two of us here, and it's a hell of a day to stop us. We're just going down to old Ensenada for a—"

"Vamos," said the Marine on Remmie's side. "Get out."

Remmie sighed, opened his door, and stepped out into the sea breeze. He backed away from the car, stared across the roof at Trevor who was doing the same. Behind them, a line of cars waited, curved northward out of sight. Remmie watched for any sign from Trevor—what the fuck we're they going to do?—but the fat man's face was plain as unsalted rice. The Marines opened the doors, dug through the center console, peered beneath the seats. After a minute, both Marines nodded at them to get back in the car.

Trevor and Remmie fell into their seats. The driver's side Marine leaned down into the window. "When you go back a Estados Unidos?"

Trevor shrugged. "We're headed back tomorrow, seen-your. If we don't get too drunk."

The Marine smirked, straightened, and waved them through the checkpoint.

As they pulled away, Remmie looked up at the baby-faced Marine, saw a grim realization in his eyes. They know, Remmie thought, they know something is up with us, that we're not doing what we're telling them. But nobody stopped them, and a minute later they were accelerating onto the high-way, falling in behind cargo trucks filled with fruit and vegeta-bles, shiny SUVs carrying college coeds and their frat-brother boyfriends. Remmie looked over at Trevor, noticed the five twenties still resting on the dashboard.

Trevor steadied the steering wheel with his belly, slid the bills off the dashboard and back into his breast pocket. "What'd I say? We're good to go, like shit through a wide pipe."

"They didn't search us. Why not?"

Trevor coughed once without covering his mouth. "Funny thing," he said, "the Marines are all mixed up down here. Guy on my side, I think he wanted the cash. But the sucker on your side...I'm not so sure. I think he was on the level."

"So, one guy wants the cash, and the other—"

"Keeps an eye on him."

Remmie said, "So, you got corruption, and you got eyes on corruption. Meanwhile, you don't change a damn thing. It's just the same old shit, the status quo."

"Neighbor, that's how the world runs. You haven't figured

that out yet, I'm sorry to make it known to you. But, hell, what else is there but right keeping its eyes on wrong?"

"I guess, nothing. It's all just watching and waiting. But for nothing."

"You got it." Trevor flipped on the Mustang's radio, tuned to Mariachi.

Remmie sighed, studied the slow turn of the highway as they approached Ensenada. The sea unfolded out his window, met a foam of fluffed-up clouds in the distance. Trevor's right about all this shit, Remmie thought, the whole world is watching itself do wrong, and not a damn thing changes. An image flashed through his head then: He saw himself, a skinny young man sitting at a Blackjack table in a rundown casino room. At each seat, the green felt on the table was worn thin, a matte wooden texture showing through. Worn through by elbows, he'd thought at the time. A million sets of elbows rested on this table, waited for the world to take, take, take.

And Remmie shook off that memory, looked over at Trevor tapping his fingers to the Mariachi music coming through the Mustang's speakers. Remmie felt the square of cash in his front pocket, resting against his thigh, the five hundred dollars he'd earned that morning. He tried to imagine what ten thousand dollars looked like all together, in one bag, how it must look in the back seat of the Dodge Charger...And with Veranda Cline driving it. He saw painted fingernails on a steering wheel, red as dried blood. He smelled cheap perfume and Vaseline.

Woman, he thought. Just the word. Nothing else. Woman.

Damn it, Remmie told himself, maybe it's time for me to take, take, take.

Maybe it's my fucking turn. How about that?

Ahead of them, Ensenada grew in their windshield. Like a city rising from the sea.

13

STREETS OF A MEXICAN TOURIST TOWN:

You got your Mariachi bands walking the streets, squat guitarists in crisp pantalones and collared camisas, black-haired heads slicked back in wet sculpture. You got tamale carts, elote salesman pushing two-wheeled flat-top grills through crowds of khaki-clad country clubbers. 'Look at this, honey,' they say to their wives and college-bound kids, 'only a buck for a whole corn on the cob. And he's putting that spice stuff on it.' You got your tiny trinket shops spilling out into the cobblestone streets. All their on-sale serapes bearing the logos of American football teams, super heroes, that old skull and crossbones. Faux wood statues of Tulum and Chichén Itzá, factory-etched facades of distant Palenque. Mini-women in traditional garb, teething babies lashed to their backs, all asking how much you'll pay for a blanket, a scarf, a handkerchief, a napkin, a lone scrap of fabric. 'Make it myself, señor. My home, I make it in my hands.' And you got street side bars shelling out green iced margaritas, gimmicky restaurants called Gringo's and Pirate's Hideout and Captain Gecko's. Carne scent and hot sauce, fried pig ears and fish.

You're not hungry, but you could eat.

And Trevor Spends, the fat man pushing through the tourists, laughing in the face of a teen girl selling baseball caps from a stick the height of a building, shaking his head at a Mexican twisting balloons into vague zoo animals. "Fucking place gets worse every year," Trevor said. "One thing after another." He pushed through an American family decked out in polo shirts and tennis shorts. "First, they put in a Captain Gecko's, and next thing you know you're selling pinwheels to some prick who manages a Wells Fargo. This town used to be charming, dammit." Trevor stopped and looked back at Remmie, eyeballed him with thick sincerity. "I remember coming here when it was like a different world, a whole new life I'd never seen." He motioned at the street, sighed. "Now, it's all carnival and mockery. Fucking place shot its damn self in the foot. And for what?" He turned and kept moving down the street, Remmie close behind him. "For a few bucks when it gets warm? Hell, you might as well give blow jobs on a cruise ship. Same fucking thing, you ask me."

Remmie thought that nobody did ask Trevor. And why would they? Talk about contradiction; the guy made his money peddling real blow jobs. Who was he to talk? But Remmie stayed quiet, followed the fat man through the streets, left down a cement path between two brick buildings. They came out into a small courtyard with stone floors and a blue plastic garden table and four chairs. There was a small stone house on the opposite side of the courtyard, adjoined to both brick buildings; the house had a wooden front door and two four-pane windows on each side.

Remmie said, "What the hell is this place?"

"Buddy of mine," Trevor said. He shouted across the courtyard, "Come the fuck out if you're home, Gonzo! I got some cash with your name on it!"

"How do you know this guy?"

"Eh, I met him on a money drop about ten years ago. He's a weapons guy, gets stuff straight from the Mexican military, has a line on the pieces the cops take out of circulation."

They waited about thirty seconds before the front door opened and a wine glass shaped man moved into the courtyard. He wore a wife beater tank top yellowed around the belly, and a pair of loose, low-slung blue jeans. He was barefoot, and Remmie noticed the man's toes were thickened by fungi, no doubt a deformity enhanced from long years working in wet boots. "Trevor," the man said. He squinted his deep black eyes and scratched his double-chin. "You still fat. I thought you going for some exercise. Lose the weight, huh?"

Trevor patted his belly. "Gonzo, this here is a partner of mine. We're working together."

Remmie moved forward and shook Gonzo's callused hand. "I go by Remmie. Remmie Miken. It's nice to meet you."

The three men moved to the garden table and sat. In the table's center, a half-full bottle of silver tequila waited. Gonzo pulled out the cork, slid the bottle toward Remmie. "Half a drink, for my new friend. You with Trevor, you with me too."

Remmie smiled on one side of his mouth, lifted the bottle and sipped.

"What kind of drink, man?" Gonzo shook his head, looked at Trevor. "You bring a gay to my house, man? You not train him in tequila?"

Trevor lifted his chin at Remmie as if to say, 'better drink some more, neighbor."

Remmie shrugged, lifted the bottle again. The liquid ran smooth over his tongue, burned like hell going down his throat. He swallowed, coughed. "Jesus," he said. "Kee-rist. That stuff's like goddamn lighter fluid." He raised his eyebrows at Gonzo. "You drink that stuff for breakfast?"

Gonzo laughed. He had a sly way of laughing, like a cartoon character with a mustache might laugh. "Lunch and dinner, too. I'm drinking tequila like water. For my soul." He patted his belly twice and rested his hand over his heart. "My one true love," he said and laughed harder.

Trevor shook his head, chuckled. "Oh, buddy. I missed seeing you."

Gonzo pointed at Remmie. "Have some more while we talk."

Trevor lifted that chin again. Remmie drank.

"What you coming for, Trevor?"

Trevor adjusted his coat, sighed a deep sigh. "Well, Gonzo. Me and Remmie here—we're on a kind of job. Looking for a girl we lost up in San Diego."

"Some whore ran out on you?"

"You got that right," Trevor said. "And she took something of mine."

"Money, huh?"

"That's it. Some money."

Remmie took another long pull from the bottle. He felt something primal stir in his belly.

"You want me ask all my friends if they seen this girl?" Gonzo's eyes stayed on Remmie, even while he spoke to Trevor. "See what they say at the cantina?"

"That might help. Something else we need though."

"Ah," Gonzo said and nodded. "Always some more, huh?"

"Need a couple pistols for the trip. None of that Chinese

crap. American-made, if you got it." Trevor sniffed hard through his plump nose, watched Gonzo watching Remmie.

Remmie drained more of the tequila, set the bottle on the table.

"You like it?" Gonzo's eyes pried at Remmie.

Remmie said, "Goes down smooth, but it burns where it should."

"Like salsa." Gonzo grinned. "The best kind. Es mejor." He looked at Trevor and said, "I can get you some guns, but this girl—must be some good money in finding her."

"That's right."

Gonzo thought for a minute, studied both of them with patience. He seemed to make a decision, let loose a drawn-out and noisy yawn. He reached out and pushed the tequila bottle toward Remmie again. "You stay here for while," he said. "Take a siesta. About the money..." He settled his black eyes on Trevor. "How much you going to give me?"

14

THE TEQUILA PUT REMMIE TO SLEEP, not to mention all the lost hours from the long night and morning; Gonzo let him snooze on a couch in the little stone house's kitchen area. When Remmie woke after a dreamless sleep, he couldn't tell what time of day it was. He felt refreshed, like he'd been run through a cool stream. What'd he get? Four, five hours of shut-eye? On the stove in the small kitchen, a pot was boiling. Remmie stood and looked inside—beans. Go figure, he was hungry again. If he kept eating like this, tacos and beans and tequila, he and Trevor would make a proper duo, fat and curvy cut-outs of each other.

Remmie saw his blue jeans draped across the couch, ironed it looked like, and a button-down Hawaiian-style shirt made from flowing fabric. Blue flowers over beach sand and ocean. Not silk, but something like it. His black t-shirt was missing. He pulled the blue jeans on over his dirty white underwear—if only they washed those for him—and draped the shirt over one shoulder. It was humid in the house with the stove on and, from what he could see out the window, a low cloud cover moved in on Ensenada. He stepped out into the courtyard; nobody at the blue table save for the empty tequila bottle.

Trevor and Gonzo must have put that bottle to bed.

But where were they?

Remmie checked down the dark alley with its high brick walls—nothing but shadows there, silhouettes moving past on the distant street. Back in the house, Remmie went from room to room: A bare bedroom with a mattress on the floor, a crooked dresser in one corner. A bathroom half-finished in gray stucco and red mission-style brick. The toilet was missing a top seat. Remmie urinated, flushed. The sink wasn't working so he wiped his hands on his jeans. One other room in the place, a ramshackle office with a metal desk, an old typewriter, and two locked file cabinets. The desk drawers were also locked. Remmie imagined Trevor went out for a bite to eat. That kind of action suited the man. Took Gonzo with him, probably. But Remmie didn't want to leave the house and courtyard, find himself turned around in Mexico looking for a fat man in a suit.

So he lay back down on the couch and smelled the detergent scent of the Hawaiian shirt.

About twenty minutes later, the house phone on the kitchen counter rang.

"Hello?" Remmie was in the house, so why not answer? "Bueno."

"Who is this?"

"Remmie, my new friend. Is Gonzo, amigo."

Remmie said, "Where'd you go? Is Trevor with you?"

"I'm taking Trevor for a dinner. You coming too."

"Put Trevor on, I want to hear what he has to say." The

phone line buzzed, clicked.

Trevor's voice came over the line. He sounded to Remmie like he might be drunk. "Neighbor. Amigo. What choo doing, mang?"

"You left me here...Where are you guys?"

"I ever tell you," Trevor said, "How much I love dis Meh-hee-co? I ever tell you. Love me some tacos and tequila. Every time I come here, it's like a heaven on paradise—"

"Where are you, Trevor?"

"Place on the street. By the ocean, lots of tequila."

"What's the name, Trevor?"

"No name bar," he said.

"How fucking drunk are you, fat man?" Remmie started to wonder then about Gonzo. Gonzo, who knew from Trevor and Remmie showing up: There must be a lot of money up for grabs, maybe more than he'd seen in a long while. More than he'd ever seen in one place. Like it was with Remmie. The same. The two of them hanging onto Trevor, trying to get to the money and, for Remmie, to the girl at the end of the line—Veranda Cline.

"Come and get some drinks, amigo." Trevor coughed, gargled, swallowed something alcoholic. "Let's have us a good time, a good night."

"Trevor, we're supposed to be after Veranda. You asking about the Dodge, the girl?"

"They seen her, amigo. Gonzo seen the girl." A shout went up from the bar, drowned out Trevor's voice. After a moment, he said, "Come on down, amigo. Get some tequila."

Trevor shook his head, shrugged the Hawaiian shirt onto his shoulders, buttoned the top two buttons. "Listen, Trevor, stay where you are—I'll be there as soon as I can find it. Just hold on and I'll find you." He finished buttoning the shirt, listened for Trevor's reply.

"No name bar," Trevor said. And that was it.

The line went dead and Remmie finished buttoning his new shirt. He went into the bathroom, studied himself in the mirror. Not bad for a fry cook on the lam. He looked like a high-powered executive gone casual, a guy so made he could unmake himself.

The look suited Remmie.

He went back into the kitchen, ran some water through his hair, stirred the beans in the pot. There was nothing more to do after that; he walked out of the house, across the courtyard, and vanished into the dark embrace of the long alley.

15

THE RAIN CAME ON AS REMMIE walked the cobblestone streets searching for his fat, drunk boss. Hard rain, like diamonds falling in thick facade. The street vendors shouted at each other, packed away Chinese-made toys and cheap clothing, hot dogs and uncooked corn, disappeared as if they were phantoms of the country. Tourists trotted past Remmie with cheap umbrellas and plastic-bag ponchos. Water seeped through his work boots and drenched him through his new shirt. He stepped up to a sidewalk bar and asked for a margarita on the rocks, drained it with a grimace, paid the bartender in wrinkled one-dollar bills. "You seen a fat man in a suit?"

The bartender shook his head. Nope.

Okay, so Remmie ambled down the empty street, peered into restaurant after restaurant as he made his way to the boardwalk. Still, no Trevor. But once he reached the boardwalk, and as he smelled the dead-fish smell of so many West

Coast port cities, he saw a blinking neon sign. In hot pink and green, the sign said: 'No Name Bar—Beer and Girls You Can Trust.' Well, Remmie thought, that sort of—kind of—makes sense. Given the way things have gone the past day or so. He trotted up the boardwalk and dodged into the bar's front door.

It, too, was a tourist place. The lower level had a square bar with a kitchen at its center. Women bartenders in low-cut tank tops circled line cooks in their stove pipe chef hats and black coats. The tables surrounding the bar were mostly full, couples smooching each other and smiling over chips and salsa. Again, no Trevor. No Gonzo. Up the stairs then, past a short waitress with her mascara running down teary cheeks. A tiny, crying girl on a staircase in rainy Mexico? Remmie thought he must be in a movie. At the top of the stairs, his suspicions were confirmed. And this, he thought, was the moment when the big actor makes his case for the golden statue. Remmie pried the wet Hawaiian shirt from his shoulders and shivered.

Trevor was standing atop a wobbly table, his tie loose and slung over a shoulder, one dress shoe missing. His face was shiny and red, like a used car salesman deep into his midday bottle. He held one hand aloft, a fat finger pointed at the rain-tapped ceiling.

Gonzo sat at the table, a half-eaten meal before him.

The dining room, full this early in the evening, was packed with collared shirts and pretty dresses. But the faces above those articles of clothing were filled with fear.

Trevor stomped on the table with his only shoe and said, "I asked for a steak done medium rare. Now, what in the fuck are you people thinking, bringing me a goddamn flank steak with flavor like a paper bag? This is America, dammit. Land of the free and the brave—I ask for a mid-rare steak and that's what I fucking deserve."

At the table, his arms crossed, Gonzo shook his head. "No America here, Trevor. Es Baja, amigo. Different place for you, my friend."

"The hell it is," Trevor said. "The fucking hell it is. If I don't get the steak I want, I'm going to shoot the fuck out of this place." Trevor pulled a black pistol from his waistband, pointed it at a few tables.

The crowd groaned. A few women screamed.

Remmie didn't know what to do. It was apparent to him that Trevor was running somehow into a darkness of his own making. He'd seen this kind of thing before; hell, he'd done it himself. Was still doing it. But Remmie figured the cops would put an end to this soon enough.

"You want me to shoot you, motherfuckers!" Trevor fired the gun through the roof. Rain poured through and fell on the floor like piss from an old man's penis. "I will, dammit. I'll shoot every last one of you! Don't you tell me what's America and what's not! I know America when I see it, damn you! I know my own fucking country!" He lowered the pistol at an older couple in a far corner. The man's white mustache bristled. His wife screamed, reached up and yanked at her frizzy hair. "The two of you go first," Trevor said.

Remmie felt himself shoved out of the way. Three men in dark suits rushed past him. None brandished guns, but all three shoved Gonzo to the floor, grabbed Trevor by his tree trunk legs and brought him down with thunderous force onto the table. They dragged him onto the floor with the last of Gonzo's meal. The plate shattered, and uneaten black beans cushioned Trevor's head as it slapped the floor. "No, dammit! I want to shoot a mother—"

Trevor was silenced by a sweeping right hook from one of the dark suits.

"Silencio, gordo," the dark suit said. He punched Trevor again. Then once more.

The gun flopped from Trevor's hand. He passed out with the final blow.

A dark suit picked up the gun, shoved it into his coat. All three men dragged Trevor by his feet from the dining area, past Remmie, and down the stairs without a thought for injury. Remmie heard Trevor's head bumping hard against the steps as he descended. When the men reached the first floor, they rested for a moment before yanking Trevor's unconscious body out of sight. Remmie scratched the back of his neck, looked back at the stunned dining room.

Gonzo was slowly getting to his feet. He brushed off his loose-fitting jeans, straightened his shirt, ran a hand through his short black hair. He cleared his throat and, in good time, noticed Remmie. "Ah, my new friend," Gonzo said. "I'm glad for seeing you. You made it. Come, come," He said with a flare of his hand. "Me and you, we must start drinking."

Start? Shit, it looked like all the drinking was already done.

Remmie stepped forward, righted one of the upended chairs. He pried at the wet Hawaiian shirt again, but its clingy fabric still stuck to his shoulders like tissue paper. The rain poured in through the hole in the roof. The dining crowd went back to eating. It was as if nothing had happened. Remmie shrugged and sat heavily in the wooden chair. He said, "They serve bourbon in Baja? I think I need a nice dose of redneck medicine."

16

NO BOURBON IN NO NAME BAR, but they had aged tequila, and plenty of it.

Remmie was on his third dose, listening to Gonzo ramble on and on about some weird real estate deal, when one of the dark suits appeared at their table. Remmie hadn't thought about Trevor. Gonzo told him the dark suits would let Trevor sleep, and that was it. But the dark suit reappearing reminded him: Oh, yeah. Somewhere in this shit hole there's a fat crook sleeping off a bender.

The dark suit pointed at Remmie's glass and said, "You like some more, amigo? Come down to the office. We got the best kind down there. Got some man who wants to say hello. To you, amigo."

He and Gonzo stood, followed the dark suit down the staircase, left through a short hallway, past a sweaty room where two squat women washed dishes, and into a grungy office about the size of a donut shop. Trevor was asleep on a ratty couch against a far wall. Closer to the door, one dark suit sat behind a battered wooden desk, another sat atop it, one leg crossed over the other. The third dark suit—Remmie and Gonzo's guide—leaned against the closest wall and grinned. The man behind the desk wore a thick goatee, well-trimmed with a hint of gray on the right side of his face. The other two were clean-shaven; Remmie thought the men might be brothers. Or cousins. He studied Trevor for injuries, but the fat man looked normal, like he needed to sleep through a bad dream, but that was all.

"We didn't hurt Trevor," said the man behind the desk. "We know him well, from his many years as a burro. Sometimes, Trevor, he needs a little—how do you say it—steam blowing off?"

Remmie shrugged. "I just met the man myself. Last night, matter of fact."

Goatee nodded thoughtfully. "Trevor always looking for a pal, huh?"

"I guess. I mean, I don't hardly know the man."

Gonzo grunted and cleared his throat. He was drunk, but not stumbling. "What you want, Rico? These men just coming to Ensenada for a good time. It's all for them. That's it."

Rico scratched his facial hair. "I never known Trevor to come for nothing but money. Or guns. Sometimes, he come down here for some drugs. Most of the time, it's the money." He stared for a long time at Remmie, raised his eyebrows. "Which one is it?"

Remmie looked at Gonzo who nodded with drunk imprecision.

Gonzo said, "Might as well tell him. Or they make you." He shot glances at the dark suits, scratched the underside of his lard-rubbed chin. "They make you hurt. They make you talk."

Remmie peeled at the Hawaiian shirt again. It was dry now, smooth across his shoulders and back. This doesn't feel like paradise Remmie, does it? He said, "We're looking for a girl in a used Dodge Charger. White girl, pretty, real name's Veranda, but she might be going by something else."

Rico said something in machine gun Spanish to his brother-cousins. Both men shook their heads, shot back brief responses. Remmie didn't catch a word.

"We heard of this girl," Rico said. "What you going to do to her?"

Remmie thought: What I'm going to do is shoot the fat man sleeping on the couch, bury him somewhere in the desert. I'm going to convince the girl that I loved her from the minute I saw her face. I'm going to take her back home, or maybe far, far away, and I'm going to marry her in a shotgun wedding. Have us a kid or two. What I'm going to do is kill the fat man, steal the girl and the money, start my fucked-to-hell life all over again. Live it like I should have lived it. But Remmie said, "We're supposed to bring the girl back to a guy in San Diego. She belongs to him." It pained Remmie to say it like that, but he knew that was how people like Rico reasoned. It was all about who belonged to who. "Girl ran out on the man, and he wants her back. You know this kind of story. Real tragic stuff."

Rico smirked. "It's not just about the girl, no?"

Remmie paused, looked at Gonzo again. Another brief, uncertain nod. Maybe you shouldn't tell, but why sign up for a beating? Remmie said, "There's some money involved—I think it's around ten grand."

"And how much you supposed to get?"

"Trevor said a thousand. Plus, the five hundred I got for last night." Remmie shifted his feet, tried not to look or feel desperate in front of these men who, he imagined, might find it a sign of weakness. Fifteen hundred bucks? It wasn't get-rich-quick money. Hell, it was barely a month or two of rent. Some beers at the pub. "That's more than I make a week. Shit, two weeks."

"If I tell you where the girl is, how to get her, how much you give us?"

"We already know where the girl is. It's just..." Remmie looked at Trevor; his mouth was open and a light snore came from his throat, like a lawnmower thinking about starting. "We got a little hung up. That's all. I mean, we appreciate the offer and everything—"

"You telling me I don't get no piece?"

Remmie should not be the one talking to this Rico character. He knew that much. What the hell should he say? Guy was pushing in on him and Trevor. Shit, guy was pushing in on Leo Action. And from what Trevor said, the stories he told, Leo Action wouldn't have it. Most of all, the guy was pushing in on Veranda Cline and Remmie's...hopes and dreams? Jesus, man. What kind of son of a bitch are you? This girl doesn't know you; she could be sickened by your fucking presence. No, Remmie thought. I know love when I see it, when I feel it. Me and Veranda, we're meant to—

Fuck. Was he going crazy?

Damn, Remmie thought, no matter how far you go, you can't get away from your own stupidity.

From the couch, his eyes still closed, Trevor spoke like the dead. There was a slight slur in his speech: "I guess I can call Leo Action, let him know his old buddy Rico Castillas wants in on this whole thing. Hell, he might even throw you a bone, ask you for a little help. Then again, Leo don't always like to hear about folks crushing in on his girls. Kind of possessive like that, he is."

Silence filled the office. Rico adjusted his black tie, fiddled with it, cursed. He yanked hard and the tie came away from his shirt—it was a clip-on. He tossed it onto the desk, settled back in his chair. "Nice of you to join us, burro. We was just talking about the girl—"

"What you could do, Rico, is you could get my friend here a gun. See, we might need it for the rest of this job. You know what kind of work I'm talking about."

Remmie rolled his tongue in his mouth. Beside him, Gonzo breathed hard through his nose. Trevor's eyes were still closed. He looked at peace. Rico nodded at the brother-cousin closest to Remmie. The man reached into his coat, came out with a sleek looking handgun. He held it out, barrel pointed at the floor, pistol grip facing Remmie.

Rico said, "A friend of the burro is a friend of mine."

He nodded at Remmie—take it, gringo.

Remmie reached out and took the pistol. In his best Spanish, he said, "Muchas gracías."

17

"RICO CASTILLAS, EL JEFE-TITO. That little bastard tried to put you under the gun, neighbor," Trevor said while he huffed along the cobblestone street toward Gonzo's stone courtyard. Remmie followed close behind, Gonzo stepping topsy-turvy behind them both—still drunk. The streets were wet with the hot sheen of rain, and the bars had new life; Mariachi music spewed from open windows, intermixed with boisterous laughter and the shouts of drunkards. Trevor stopped to catch his breath, started moving forward after he suppressed the wheeze in his throat. "I knew Rico since the late nineties. He was just a half-price coyote back then, smuggling Guatemalans in through Otay Mesa. Little bastard couldn't so much as grow a peach-fuzz goatee back then. Probably never had a hard-on neither. Not until I came along. Me and Leo paid for the girl that popped Rico's Mexican cherry. You fuckin' believe that? I paid for that fucker's first tush and he's trying to push in on me?" The three men crossed the avenida, forged through a cadre of mustached Mexicans selling those metallic helium balloons. Trevor talked like he'd never been drunk, like he was fresh from a long night's sleep. Maybe that was what annoyance did to him. Or anger. "Let me tell you, if that tiny brown bastard thinks he can muscle me, Leo Action's hard muscle, he's the stupidest cocksucker on the peninsula. Shit, the goddamn planet. And he's sitting there all high and mighty in that joint with his illiterate cousins...Them two taco disposals couldn't read a cereal box with a fuckin' tutor. I'm talking Spanish here. Their mother-fucking-tongue."

They passed the sidewalk bar where Remmie got his afternoon margarita, pushed on through a puddled sidewalk, reached sight of the two buildings that formed the alleyway to Gonzo's courtyard.

"I met Rico Castillas and he called himself Ricky—you fuckin' believe that? Like the kid was an extra on a fifties TV show. It was me who got him into the real money. Got him off that coyote bit. You know what a coyote is? A goddamn scrounger, a predator of pure and simple luck. A coyote gets a good dinner, he won the fuckin' lottery." Remmie followed Trevor into the dark alley, felt Gonzo just behind him.

Trevor kept up his tirade. "You take a brown bastard and put him on the money, you expect he's going to keep that in his thoughts. I guess that isn't how Rico Castillas works, no?" The alley went dark, a small tunnel headed toward a square of vague light. Trevor's voice bounced against the stone walls. "I guess little brown Rico Castillas got too big to pay back the men who—"

A blast—unmistakable gunfire—came as they reached the courtyard; it pushed Trevor, fat ass Trevor, back against the stone wall, back into the darkness of the alley. His voice oomphed from his throat, died somewhere in the space between stone and sky. He fell forward, turned onto his back. Putting a hand to his belly, it came away red, wet with blood and guts.

Behind Remmie, Gonzo said, "Dios-fucking-mío."

Trevor's body shuddered. He tried to speak but nothing came from between his lips. He was all hot air and pain.

Remmie brought out the black pistol—he had it shoved down the front of his waistband, hidden beneath the loose Hawaiian shirt—and pointed it at the invisible shooter.

Another shot sounded in the courtyard, smacked the wall above Trevor's fish-mouthing face.

Remmie flinched, tightened his grip on the pistol and, without thinking one sad or tired thought, fired the gun until it wouldn't—no, couldn't—fire any goddamn more.

18

BEFORE REMMIE COULD STOP his sorry-ass self, he was running after the shooter, crossing the stone courtyard and leering after a thin, black-clad grasshopper of a fucker. The shooter dodged the alcove shielding the stone house from the fledgling moonlight, leaped atop a low cinder-brick wall. He was on the roof in an instant, a human insect with feet like suction cups.

"Hey, stop!" Remmie hopped onto the wall, saw black fabric vanish over the house's far side. "I'm going to shoot if you don't stop!" Shoot? Shit...Shoot nothing. Remmie didn't have a round left in his gun. Fuck, I'm going to have to go after him. Remmie pulled himself onto the roof, scraped his right hand because it was still closed over the pistol. Blood ran between brick and stone, made Remmie's fingers slippery on the warm steel.

Gonzo shouted from below, "Shoot him, cabrón!"

Remmie ran across the roof, reached the far side. An

adjacent alley, this one wider and flanked by small homes, ran east away from him. Through the useless light of early evening, Remmie saw a thin figure, like a shadow, moving down one side of the alley, running hard toward the street where traffic zoomed in both directions. Remmie lifted the pistol, aimed as best he could, pulled the trigger. Nothing but a click. The shadow twitched, stumbled, fell. "Shit," Remmie said, "Maybe I already got the fucker." But a moment later the shadow was kneeling, standing, running hard toward the far street, a black stain favoring one leg. Remmie knew he had no chance to catch the guy. He pulled the trigger again, but all that came, like he expected, was an audible click.

For the sheer nasty hell of it, he fired the empty pistol twice more.

● ● ●

In the courtyard, Remmie kneeled beside Trevor.

"Got me, huh?" Trevor's breath came rapid, shot sparks of red blood across his broad chin. "Son of a bitch hit me where it hurts. Where it don't come out from."

"Don't talk, okay?"

Trevor's eyes shined against the evening. It was clear he was in pain, that he was headed for a shock state. His chest was mangled, bloody and splashed with torn cloth and skin. His tie was cut off at the knot. Remmie didn't see Gonzo, imagined he was calling for help from the house phone.

"Don't say a thing," Remmie said. "Gonzo, where are you?" He looked back to the house, saw a light flash on in the kitchen. For some reason, Remmie thought: Don't forget to stir the beans. They'll burn the bottom of the pot if you don't stir, stir, stir. Fuck the beans, man. Trevor was dying in Remmie's fucking arms. "Trevor, do me a favor—hold on. We're going for some help. A doctor."

"I'm dying, neighbor." Blood ran over his bottom lip. "Ambushed, amigo. Fuck. Fuck."

"Just shut up, Trevor. Let me—"

Trevor gripped Remmie's shirt, yanked him to the ground. Blood and hot alcohol breath hit Remmie's left ear.

Trevor said, "Leo wanted to kill the girl. He planned on it. All the way back. But now we know she's got guts. He's got to kill her. Don't you see that? Me, I got to do it."

Remmie tried pulling away, couldn't escape Trevor's death grip.

"I was supposed to kill you," Trevor said. "Because you saw what I did to the pimp, what I was going to do to the girl. Because you knew everything. Because Leo said, and what Leo says—"

"You'd fucking kill me?" Remmie twisted his head, came eye to eye with Trevor. "You would fucking kill me after all this, us going after the girl—"

"It's what Leo says." Trevor's voice went high, shrieked. "Leo says it and I do it. That's all I ever did. Leo tells me, and I do. You get it? Don't you see? Don't you understand a goddamn fucking thing? The pimp. The girl. The fucking cop from up north. All the people before that. Them girls and the kids down off Euclid. Fuck. You see it, right? I'm dying." Blood surged from Trevor's mouth, made him smack his lips like a man eating too much syrup. "I had to do you, but I didn't want to." The hole in his chest seemed black and too deep for reality. "I don't know why, but I liked you and...shit."

Remmie yanked Trevor's hand from his collar, straightened. He looked back at the house. Another light came on, Gonzo shouted something inaudible at the night. Looking back at Trevor, Remmie had a sudden familiar urge. He left the pistol laying on the cold stones, took his bloody hand and placed it over Trevor's mouth. The fat man's breath was light, almost absent.

Remmie closed his eyes. So simple to do this, he thought. It's a gift. My god, he's dead anyway. And he was planning to kill you. Should have done it before, after his boss made the play. But he couldn't do it. That's how death gets in, Remmie thought, like a good friend you don't expect. He's warm until it all...goes... cold. Trevor shivered, shook. "Quiet, fat man," Remmie whispered. "Let the world shrink way. It's better like this. No knives. No needles. No more whores or gambling or—"

"Down here!" Gonzo shouted from behind Remmie.

When he turned, Remmie knew Gonzo hadn't seen what he was doing. He was waving at two men passing the far entrance to the alleyway. Remmie turned back and saw the men enter the dark mouth made by the high stone walls. He shrugged, lifted his bloody hand from Trevor's mouth.

The men ran toward them.

Gonzo's hand gripped Remmie's shoulder, pried at him. Remmie grunted, stood slowly, began to back away—looking down at Trevor, he caught movement: The fat man was still breathing.

19

PAINT THE ROOM RED, the kitchen table, the pastel tile floor. Get it on the walls, on two sets of grasping brown hands. Kitchen forks and pocket knives. A spoon digging like a rounded tooth. One steel bead of gut shot after another clinking into a tin coffee cup. Click. Clink. Clink. And on into the wee hours, until the gray morning seeps in around the window sill. Voices, screams...Last little moans of pain, like a crow diving into a ravine.

Death. Near death. Not-quite-yet-death.

Remmie tried to sleep on the couch in the living room while the two men—older, gruff, wearing loose-fitting collared shirts—dug the gut shot from Trevor's well-fed belly. It occurred to Remmie he'd seen more blood in the past forty-eight hours than in his entire life. He did not want to think too hard about what this foretold. After what Trevor told him, Remmie knew his blood, his body and existence, was on the menu for consumption.

Not the most savory of offerings.

At least, not to Remmie.

As the morning grew around them, started to pry at the windows beneath the stone house's awning, Trevor's moans gave way to aimless ramblings. "Leo wants the girl," he said. "Wants to eat her up, make her what she isn't. Leo wants it all. Everything I ever had. Leo Action eats the whole world. The whole damn thing. Leo action ate the whole goddamn world and I never got a piece."

And Gonzo, now sober, gripped Trevor's hand, massaged his fat knuckles. "Quiet, Trevor. Better saying nothing to get you in trouble. Better your heart keep pumping sangre, keep going."

As the dawn came, Remmie stood and watched the older men work. They did not have medical training, he knew. Not formal medical training. But he could see they had pried bullets and whatever else from men's bodies before—lots and lots of bullets from lots and lots of bodies. It all came out, the steel. Or lead.

Clink. Clink. Clink.

And Remmie dipped two fingers into the tin coffee cup and came out with one of the round pellets, held it to the light, studied it.

Trevor spoke, "You see what kind of thing I got us into, neighbor."

Remmie dropped the pellet into the coffee cup.

Clink.

The two men with the prying hands kept at it, worked in silence.

"I see it's trouble," Remmie said. "But I knew that when I said I'd do it."

"And you saw the girl," Trevor said. He nodded slightly. "The picture." His face was pale, the skin like sour cream spread across hardwood. Purple lips kept talking, though no words came through them. He coughed, spit blood onto a napkin embroidered with pink-flowering cacti.

Gonzo groaned. "Silencio, burro. Let my friends doing their work."

"What about the picture?"

The men stopped for a long minute, whispered among themselves, started prying nearer Trevor's waistline. He was naked to the waist, his chest speckled with gut shot; it was his belly that took the true hit. It was a mangled lump of fat, guts, churned up skin and blood.

Trevor groaned and said, "I could tell... You wanted the girl for yourself."

Gonzo's eyes shot to Remmie.

Remmie said, "How could you tell that?"

"Starving eyes never lie."

"Burro," Gonzo said. "No more talking to this—"

"You want the money, too." Trevor groaned again, yelped as fingers yanked gut shot from his belly button. "That what you want?"

Remmie thought for a long time; finally, he nodded.

Trevor smiled, showed blood-stained teeth.

Remmie said, "I had a whole life before this. Something good, too. I fucked it up. I threw it away and it just—I don't know how to say it. But I lost it all, just gave it the fuck away."

"I know what you mean, neighbor. I hear you."

"Go on and die then." Remmie knew it was cold, hard, horrible. But he fucking meant it.

Trevor started to chuckle, yelped with pain.

The room smelled of silence and blood then, like the bathroom where Trevor cut the pimp into pieces. Like the alley where they tossed the body into the bay. Death has a scent.

One of the gruff men clapped his bloody hands together twice. "No más," he said and ran a finger across his throat. Gonzo nodded. The men left the house. Remmie heard their footsteps enter the alley on the stone walkway, fade, disappear. Again, the room was silent.

"You think Leo's gonna come for us?"

Trevor squinted at Remmie. "It wouldn't be a good story if he didn't. Hell, it wouldn't be a goddamn thing if he didn't. This whole world would be a lie… if he… if he let you go."

"And the girl?"

"Her too."

Gonzo shook his head. The Mexican's hair was caked to his cheeks from sweat and effort. He said, "I think maybe Rico Castillas shot you, Trevor. He killed you, burro. What you want me to do?"

Trevor breathed with harsh intakes of breath. Air like razorblades. He shivered. "Bury him face down, the selfish little prick," Trevor said.

Remmie cleared his throat. "And what about you?"

Trevor's fat hands clenched into fists. He coughed twice. Blood dribbled onto his chin. "Put me where…" His face shriveled with pain. "Put me where I can watch the…" Staggered breaths. More blood. "…Watch the sea," he said. "Where I can watch the—"

The fat man was gone.

Gonzo sighed. "Pinche muerte," he said. "Perro de la vida."

Remmie thought only of Veranda Cline's face. Her thin profile on the cell phone screen was imprinted in his mind. He was blind to all else. He took a thoughtful breath, pursed his lips. "Más tequila," he said. "Por favor." Again, in his best Spanish.

20

MID-MORNING IN ENSENADA. Remmie steered the black Mustang through the cobblestone and dirt streets. He rolled through a stop sign, endured, with indifference, Gonzo's groan in the passenger seat. No Mexican cop was going to arrest them for rolling through a stop sign.

But then again, Remmie figured he better not push his sorry luck.

Besides, they had the fat man—his body—in the rear seat, rolled up like a burrito in a mold-stained shower curtain. You make do with what you can find.

Remmie, of course, thought about chopping Trevor into manageable pieces—hell, he'd seen it done before—but Gonzo wouldn't have it.

"Burro," Gonzo said, "goes to the Earth like a prince."

Remmie shook his head and thought: Some fucking prince.

For Remmie, it was funny to be here on a weekday.

Cruising Ensenada in a back Mustang. A dead body in the back seat. Some paunchy Mexican shyster riding shotgun. Like he was on vacation in a screwball Hollywood comedy. Something a shit-for-brains writer might put together while he's deep in a bender, staying in a whore-favoring motel outside of Pahrump, Nevada. A hack screenplay deal.

Oh, the places you'll go, huh?

"You make it to the highway over there." Gonzo waved at a dirt on-ramp.

Remmie steered them through dust sifting from a semi-truck carrying strawberries, accelerated onto the highway, passed a long mile of street vendors peddling firewood, over-ripe mangoes, cell phone chargers, and the occasional icy coconut liquado. The thing that killed him about Mexico: It seemed like everybody was selling something, and there were plenty of people buying. But shit, if so many people bought, how come people were still selling? And then he remembered his job flipping burgers and drenching French fries in fat. You peddle whatever gets another payment to the rent man—that's the goddamn way it is the world over; Remmie was smart enough to see that.

Just not smart enough to escape it.

But this Veranda Cline...Remmie sees her picture and all of the sudden he's seeing a whole new world, a blue heaven opening up before him. Like it must be walking into a Vegas casino for the first time—all that green scratch waiting for the taking. What was it about her? Remmie couldn't say. He only knew the woman and her image, and the idea of her, had him by the throat and the heart and the fucking balls. Why? What was it? Not her looks. Remmie had been with beautiful women—your all-American types, right—and that couldn't be all there was to it. That wasn't enough. No, sir. Some type of draw, a magnetism. A goddamn force to be reckoned with inside him.

What? What? What?

And Remmie kept repeating the name—Veranda-Veranda-Veranda—inside his head.

You're fucking obsessed, Remmie.

Gonzo's voice burned through his thoughts: "Mr. Remmie, cuidado!"

Remmie swerved the Mustang across two dirt lanes, missed an old man pedaling a tricycle stacked with off-green watermelons. He heard curses in Spanish, a whirligig horn behind him. "Fucking shit, the hell is that guy doing in the road?" Remmie righted the Mustang, throttled into a curve that led from the town toward gray-green humpback mountains in the distance.

Gonzo slammed both hands on the dashboard. "This not your country, you motherfucker."

"You think I want to kill a watermelon salesman?"

"I think you bringing me nothing but hell and death."

Remmie raised his eyebrows, checked the rearview mirror. Nobody on their tail—he wondered if it was Rico Castillas who killed Trevor. Could have been Leo Action for all Remmie knew. Anyway, they were followed by a caravan of semi-trucks and dumpy looking sedans. No black Crown Vics or Dodge Chargers or whatever-the-hell halfway gangsters drove.

Gonzo said, "We got to go a checkpoint later."

"The fuck you mean?"

"Mexican Marines. Bad asses."

"So?"

"They gonna search the car, gringo."

Remmie chanced a look at the big man heavy-dead in the rear seat. "What are we going to do with...Trevor?" Sure, Remmie wanted to chop the man up, but that was to make things easier.

He still felt the man deserved a semi-proper burial.

"What you mean?"

"All this bury me by the sea, bullshit. You in for that?" Remmie steered into the oncoming lane, powered the Mustang past another dusty semi-truck. This one was loaded with apricots.

"In two miles, take the left. We throw him in the canal, where the farm waters go."

"Excuse me? I thought you called him a prince of the fucking Earth. Now you want to dump the man in a ditch?"

Gonzo rolled his eyes, stared out the window. It was all scrubland turning to cultivated crops, artichokes and watermelons and whatever else the white man eats. "I don't like it to cut a man's body. What can I say? I don't like it that kind of work, that thing. I used to do this… Before I make it out. Power tools. It's no good. Get rid of him before going the checkpoint."

"You mean you want to dump the man? But you won't chop his ass into pieces?"

"In canal, where the—"

"Fucking farm waters, I know." Remmie couldn't believe it. Gonzo wanted to dump the man and leave him. It didn't matter how they did it, only that they didn't have the body when they made the checkpoint. He felt nauseous then, fed up with life and Mexico and the dead. Fed up with bodies. Since he crossed the border with Trevor, shit had gone haywire, and not in the best way. He was closer to Veranda, but farther. He was more poor, but maybe about to get rich. He was nothing and everything, all of it at once. Remmie didn't respond to Gonzo. Instead, he floored the Mustang, turned left at the next dirt road, fish-tailed toward the distant, snake-like shape of the irrigation canal.

• • •

It was hot. Remmie sneezed as the dust entered his nose and lungs. His Hawaiian shirt, like the night before, stuck to his shoulders and biceps. He peeled at it, thought about going shirtless. Flat acreage of expansive farmland lay in front of them, just beyond a canal of oil-black water. In the distance, a farmer ran a green tractor through what looked to Remmie like berries, but he couldn't tell from this far away—Gonzo was coughing up a lung, all the dust hitting him too. He hacked a few times into his fist, rubbed a thumb across both eyes. Remmie shrugged. "You want to throw the man here, not find a better place? Something more...secret?"

Gonzo cleared his throat and said, "Nothing secret in Me-hi-co. We do it here. Nobody care, gringo. Nobody know a goddamn thing." The man stood there like a bereft and unfit general, his loose collared shirt flapping in the hot wind and his black hair dangling like a crooked wig.

Remmie decided not to argue. Yes, the farmer was there in the distance, but he couldn't see what they were doing, could he? Shit, whatever. Not like anybody dared report them. Remmie knew the reputation of Mexican authorities, though he wasn't sure the accusations were true. He thought back to the Marines Trevor tried to bribe, how the one stared through them as if they were cellophane. Not the type of man to corrupt himself—you knew that from the Marine's eyes. Should be more like him in this world. Or, depending who you were and what you did, way less of him. Remmie went back to the Mustang, opened the driver's side door, and began to yank Trevor's body out by his arms. The big man's ass got wedged between the front and back seats; his torso toppled over the doorway onto the dirt road. "Dammit, you going to help me, or just stand there?" Remmie yanked again, failed.

As Gonzo moved to help him, Remmie heard an engine on the road. It was high-pitched and whiney, like—yep, he was right—a four-wheeler. Sure enough, a quad motorcycle appeared in a dust cloud, sped toward them without braking until the last second. The engine downshifted, whined. The vehicle slid to a stop beside the Mustang.

Remmie pinned Gonzo with a death-stare. What the fuck were they supposed to do now?

"¡Hola!" The helmet-less rider hopped off his quad, walked toward them. He was a gangly kid without a shirt, the skin on his chest burned brown with work and sun. "What you doing, man?" He said it with an American TV accent and smiled. A big goofy smile, like he was slow.

Gonzo spoke in rapid Spanish, stopped the kid in his tracks.

Remmie watched both of them while the dust settled. Here they were trying to throw a fat man in a canal and this kid comes along. More shit-for-luck down in Baja. Before they left Ensenada, Remmie stashed his bullet-less pistol beneath the driver's seat. He thought about reaching for it. Scare the kid, maybe? How else to get him out of here? Not the best idea, pulling a gun without ammunition.

Instead, he waited.

The kid lifted his hands, spoke in slow monotone to Gonzo.

Spanish phrases Remmie didn't understand.

Gonzo said, "Orale." He looked to Remmie, "This guy says we are okay here. Good place to leave the burro, huh? Cartels do it all the time."

"You mean, he's all good with it?" Fucking great. Talk about tourist attractions, huh?

"He don't give a fuck," Gonzo said. "No worries."

"Tell his ass to give us a hand then."

Gonzo chirped at him and the kid came around to help. The three of them yanked the big man's body from the Mustang, dragged him across the dirt to the canal's edge. His pants made a scratchy sound and for some reason Remmie remembered the pimp's limbs shifting in the black trash bag. Trevor's slacks came undone as they dragged him, split to reveal a wide ass with near-purple cheeks. He had a crude line tattoo of an angel on one cheek.

The canal was about ten feet down a steep grade, a thin river of dark water that ran north as far as Remmie could see. South until it reached a curve and dipped east. Water for the farms.

Gonzo crossed himself.

Remmie said, "Nice to know the big man, I guess. He was a hell of a neighbor and he wanted to pay me well. And that's something." And Remmie meant it—that was something. Too bad the Mexicans who did Trevor's surgery—if you wanted to call it that—ripped off his fat wad of cash. All Remmie had left was the 500 smackers from the pimp's disposal. He'd got that bit in the strip club, just after they crossed the border.

The skinny kid bent at the waist, pushed Trevor's body with a loud grunt.

The big body spun slowly at first, picked up speed and dust, twirled into the dark water with a loud splash. Trevor slid out into the middle of the canal, his limbs motionless, and sank slightly. He drifted south.

He was facedown.

Remmie said, "God, he was a big, big man."

"He was a son of a bitch," Gonzo said. "Amen."

The skinny kid saluted with his left hand. Flapped that goofy smile.

The body floated downstream, turned the corner out of sight.

In the far distance, the green tractor slowed, stopped. The driver climbed out of the cab, hung off the side with one arm dangling lazily. He studied what must have been the trim silhouettes of three motionless figures.

Behind them, the arching sun crossed above low desert mountains.

No princes here. No burial at sea.

Just a dead man floating down an irrigation canal, headed toward the far side of the river.

Oh, the places you'll go, huh?

● ● ●

Lots of places to go in this world—not all good places.

Nope. There's bad places and mean places and horrible places.

Where was Remmie now, driving down a two-lane Mexican highway, the sun at his back through tinted windows? Baja. The peninsula. A place full of decency and debauchery—all of it priced for the bargain-hunter, the middling American adventurer, the shoestring budget seeker. Ah, Baja. The last great road trip on Earth. Make the most of it then, Remmie, and stop mourning Trevor and the pimp and the lost girl...And the money.

"Checkpoint coming up," Gonzo said.

"What about the pistol?"

"La pistola? Ah, I forget. Throw it out the window."

Up ahead, the highway curved between two hills, passed a sign for a winery. Remmie noticed, a few miles back, vineyards started to emerge from the farmland, gradually overtook the more practical crops. Mexican wine country: Who thought that one up? "Get rid of the pistol? Fuck you," Remmie said. "Not with that bastard Rico Castillas after us. I need that thing."

"You got more bullets?" Gonzo lifted his eyebrows at Remmie, smiled with half his mouth.

"I was hoping you might know where I could—"

"They take an American to jail, he has a gun. Long time, amigo."

Remmie steered the Mustang into the curve, slowed as the tires squealed. "You think I'm going after the girl without a gun? Please, I may not know how to use the thing, but I still want it. I still need it."

"Let me go after the girl for you," Gonzo said. "I find her with friends I have."

"These the same friends put Trevor in the canal?"

"That was Leo Action. Must be Leo. Rico, he's too afraid."

Remmie's eyes brushed across the rearview mirror. For all he knew, one of the dumpy, lopsided sedans could be following them, but he doubted it. If Leo Action sent a hitman, you can bet the fucker would be in a decent ride. Style points counted with people in Leo Action's line; Remmie figured that from his time with Trevor Spends. Oh, how short it was... He wondered if Gonzo was serious. "You think Leo killed the fat man then?"

He watched Gonzo's face while he worked up an answer.

Plain as pizza dough, not a damn thing to it.

"I think it must be Leo. Maybe Rico. But I think Leo. He say he need to kill you, no? He don't kill you, they kill him."

"And after that?"

"Well, I say it nice you want. They lay you down next. Put you to sleep."

"Muerte," Remmie said.

"Simón."

Oh, when death gives chase, Remmie thought. And here I am running to a woman. "You know where we turn for Puerto Santo Thomás?"

Gonzo nodded. "You still going? Turn on the dirt road coming after the big winery."

"The big winery?"

"Looking, how you say, nice? A fancy place."

"Sure, sure."

"Let's go back a Ensenada, gringo. Volvemos. I get you the girl, we split the money."

Remmie shook his head. He knew to get the money, really get it, he had to do this himself. And the girl, too—Veranda Cline. "You don't want to go?"

Gonzo sighed, spoke without looking at Remmie. "I want to see the money, sure. Keep my gringo friend safe. I do it for the burro, but..."

They came out from between the two hills, sped down a flat stretch of highway toward a boxy structure in the distance, all plywood and tin.

"You stop here, gringo? I need to take a piss."

Remmie slowed the Mustang, swung it onto the gravel shoulder, into the dirt parking lot. The plywood-tin palace was a general store with firewood, gasoline, and miscellaneous canned foods. Lots of other meaningless crap. A sign out front said the baños cost a few pesos. "Go on in," Remmie said. "I'll wait out here for you."

Gonzo looked hard at Remmie, squinted. "You don't know nothing about my country, gringo. I think we turn around, go back. Es mejor, no? Let Leo Action have the girl. What you want with her? Some kind of whore you can't find in San Diego? She just a woman, sabes?"

Just a woman—right, Remmie thought, everybody is just a woman to a man like you. He thought for a moment about his wife—former wife, that is—and told himself Gonzo was right, that all women are just women. No more, no less. Except he knew it was a lie. He knew Veranda Cline was waiting for him, wanted him, needed him. How? He didn't know, but she pulled at him like…like a hook run through his heart. Yanking, pulling, tearing. The why and the how and the where didn't matter. What mattered was that hook, that bloody point tearing at his insides.

Damn this world and its unexplainable attractions.

Damn that which rips through us.

"I told Trevor I'd help him find the girl," Remmie said. "And the Dodge Charger."

Gonzo rolled his brown eyes beneath sleepy eyelids. "And the money, no?"

"All of it."

"So, fine. I go with you."

"Your choice, pal. Stay or go. Me, I'm headed to Puerto Santo Thomás."

"Pinche fishing place. Smelling like the dead." Gonzo got out of the car, leaned in and said, "I'm coming back. Uno momentito. Wait here, okay?"

Remmie nodded. He waited until Gonzo entered the general store. Then he threw the Mustang in reverse. He backed up, flipped the transmission into drive. He throttled hard toward the highway and heard dust and gravel shoot out behind him like a shotgun blast. The tires squealed when he hit pavement and, when the dust cleared after a quarter mile, he saw Gonzo's squat figure standing in the center of the highway. He had his hands on his hips and Remmie imagined he was shaking his head.

Adíos, sucker.

After a few minutes doing seventy, Remmie saw military trucks ahead, a dozen young men with assault rifles and ski masks covering their faces.

The checkpoint.

And he still had the pistol beneath his seat.

21

REMMIE FOUND TIME, BEFORE HE REACHED the checkpoint, to take stock of his new life; and, to be sure, his new life was an outlaw life. A girl on the run and you're after her. A dead man in a canal, and he's the muscle for a halfway gangster who might be after you. And you left the one guy who knows his way around Baja behind at a ramshackle corner store. You don't even know how to buy gas, or what to do if you get pulled over by a cop. And the pistol under your seat is a problem. At the very least, it's the beginning of a problem.

The Mustang's engine droned on, ceaseless as ocean static.

Ahead, the checkpoint loomed.

A line of cars and semi-trucks stretched for a few hundred yards, led to a sandbag barricade with a beige barracks building to one side. An armed soldier stood on each side of the line of cars, asked random passengers to step out while they searched the interior of each vehicle. The other soldiers sat around a picnic table, stared at either each other or the plodding line of vehicles. It looked like random searches, but Remmie couldn't be certain.

What made them search a given car? Suspicion? A hunch? Every third or fourth as ordered?

Remmie recalled a conversation with his ex-wife:

"I know you're hiding something, Remmie. You got it written on your face."

"What's that mean?"

"It means I can see your lies in your smile, the way you blink, your fucking wrinkles."

"I'm not hiding nothing." Except Remmie was hiding something—he was hiding a hell of a lot and it had to do with gambling debts. You want to hide that stuff, you have to try hard.

"You're a liar, Remmie Miken. You always have been. You lie to me. You lie to yourself. And you can't even stop yourself...It's just part of your nature."

"You're saying I'm unreliable."

She said, "I'm saying you've been lying this whole time."

"But I haven't, I swear to—"

"Sure you have. A man who lies to himself is the worst kind of man. Can't even—"

Forget that, Remmie. You're something else now. A hero. A man going after a woman. A man after something real, something authentic, something that couldn't be a lie if it tried. And now, if your lying self was ever going to help your authentic self, this is the moment. Those soldiers are going to ask you questions. And how you answer, it'll make your life prison, or it'll make your life the open road.

The line diminished.

Remmie throttled the Mustang forward, inched toward the two soldiers.

He wiped sweat from his forehead, checked his gaze in the rearview. I look good, he thought. I look fine. I'm headed down to do some fishing. Get me a tuna or a big yellowtail. No fishing rod? I'm going to rent the sucker, you know how it is. A fishing hat, too. And some swim trunks. Less cars now. A long delay. Random thoughts and fears in the Mexican afternoon.

Four cars to go. Three. Two. You're next, Remmie.

And isn't that the same Marine from yesterday? The one who watched that bribe like a hawk? Isn't this your shit-for-luck, Remmie?

Isn't this it?

• • •

The tall Marine's eyes drilled Remmie like pistol fire. He smirked and said, "¿Adónde vamos?" He didn't blink. His partner looked into the open passenger side window.

Remmie gulped, wiped sweat from his forehead. In his best gringo-tourist voice: "I'm headed down to, a, Point-o Santo Tom-us. You know where that is? I guess they got some decent yellowtail off the coast there." Remmie showed size with his hands, looked from one Marine to the other. "They got big ones I can catch with a guide. You know what I'm talking about? Big fish. Pescado grande, eh?" Remmie rested his hands on the steering wheel, tapped his thumbs like a pianist.

The tall Marine grunted. "¿Y ayer? Yesterday? You stay where?"

"Oh, Ensenada," Remmie said. "That's one hell of a town! Margaritas con damas." He faked a jolly laugh.

The soldiers did not respond.

"We had us a nice dinner at a little cantina...Boy, those margaritas put a man on his ass, huh? I bet you boys know what I'm saying. You got a favorite place to plow through some tequila, drink the worm? Hell, maybe we can meet up, have us a—"

"¿Y tu amigo?" The tall Marine let the smirk drip away, replaced it with a plain expression too serious to challenge.

"You mean—"

"El gordo."

The bastard remembered. Remmie saw bad ass in this son of a bitch Marine, and it was coming through right this minute."You mean my pal, huh?" Remmie held out his hands again to signal a fat midsection. He patted his stomach. "Mi amigo es, uh, pain in estomago. Sabes? Too much tequila y…" Remmie made a V shape with his hands. "Long night, my friends. Noche es el…long-A." Jesus, Remmie. Way to pour on the old gringo vibe. You want them to forget you, not remember how stupid you are. You don't even know what they call the Mexican Academy Awards—stop trying to win yourself one. He finished, "No bueno, señor. No bueno."

The passenger side Marine chuckled, shot rapid Spanish at his partner.

But the other Marine kept those dark eyes on Remmie.

"Look, amigo, señor, I'm just trying to get down and have a little fishing ex—"

Remmie was interrupted by a peppering of nearby gunfire; it came fast and sporadic, like a child coughing down a long hallway. The Marines mobilized, took cover behind sandbags. The tall Marine seemed in charge, at least for the few moments before a burly Marine with a brown ski mask on jogged from the barracks. He carried a pistol pressed tight against his thigh. He conferred with the tall Marine and both men took cover, peered into the distance with field glasses. Beyond the checkpoint, the highway ran straight for a couple hundred yards, curved westward into a gully, disappeared after a low rise. The gunfire came again, but it didn't seem to have a clear origin. Remmie sensed the unease behind him, all the Mexican families huddled in their cars hoping, if the heat didn't kill them, the gunfire was an imagining. There was a long tense minute, but soon a rundown semi-truck chugged along the highway's rise, coasted down onto the straight-away; it took the driver accelerating, but the gunfire came again. A backfiring engine. The Marines shook their heads, sauntered back to the picnic table. In the line of cars, a volley of honks sounded in celebration.

The tall Marine waved Remmie through the checkpoint. He had his eyes on the line of cars as Remmie passed, but for an instant he shot a look into the Mustang.

Remmie swore he heard the Marine's voice lingering behind him:

"Cuidado, gringo," it said. "Cuidado."

22

MEXICANS DRIVE A HELL OF A LOT different than Americans do. Remmie didn't think he was being racist to think that. It was a fact and it was there for him to snatch. What he noticed was that Mexican truckers pulled along the road's shoulder—still keeping with the speed limit, mind you—and waved passenger cars through. On its face, this strategy pays. But it happened in both directions, and Remmie had two close calls with pickup trucks, near head-on collisions. Hell of a thing to die on a Mexican highway. Remmie got anxious thinking about it. His breath tugged up into his chin, and he felt a tightening in his crotch.

Every now and again, he noticed a crucifix planted on the side of the road. Often there were dead flowers and statues of the Virgin de Guadalupe, too. As he ran the Mustang south along the highway, he imagined all the dead souls lining his path. And Trevor Spends was one. Remmie saw the big man chewing hard on his eggs Benedict back in

San Diego, smacking his fat lips into each other like inner tubes. It wasn't the souls that made Remmie feel odd; for him, it was all the crosses he saw. He saw ramshackle crucifixes, stitched together with rusty nails and plywood. He saw elaborate crucifixes, like something you'd pay a craftsman to forge or sculpt. He saw crucifixes etched into the dirt with tiny stones, crucifixes drawn on fences and walls.

Crucifixes. Crucifixes. Crucifixes.

This got Remmie thinking about God. The Big Man.

The One and Only. Or so say so many.

Remmie wasn't sure about God. Once, he'd tried to talk to the man:

"You up there, listening in?"

Silence.

"Look, I've done some stupid things, but I'd like to keep my family, if that's okay."

Quiet reflection.

"I mean, shit, everybody fucks up goddammit and—oh, shit, I'm fucking sorry."

Brooding up above.

"You give me anything I can do right? I mean, fuck. I'm going to die a big zero."

Still, nothing.

And that was the extent of Remmie's religious life. Shouldn't that magnetic pull he felt toward Veranda be the same inside him when it came to God? Did everybody feel that pull when they crossed themselves, kneeled before the priest, ate the stale cracker-body of Christ? Remmie doubted it. He thought maybe religion was a long con, but that wasn't what bothered him. No, Remmie worried about the truth. If God was up there, watching Remmie's every single fuck up and screw off, what could he say to the man when he met him? I done fucked shit up? Would that be enough? It wasn't enough for Remmie's ex, for his mother, for his shit-for-brains uncle. And Remmie knew dead bodies. Hell, he'd watched a pimp get chopped to pieces. And where was God when that was going down? Taking a fucking cat nap? Yeah, Remmie thought, to hell with God if he's got nothing for me.

To hell with him. And everything else.

Except for Veranda.

And the money.

There you go again, Remmie, making yourself into a...a...a Big Fat Zero.

He decided not to look at more shrines or crucifixes or fucking rundown churches.

No more thoughts on God.

Remmie stared at the line in the center of the highway, ran it down into sunset. The road narrowed, closed in on itself as he reached a different elevation. More greenery here, a cool breeze from the valleys, vineyards rising out of the gullies, peppering the hills.

Remmie checked his rearview mirror, lurched against his seatbelt. He saw Trevor's face in the mirror, heard the man's voice echoing in his head: "Me and Leo Action, we been together for a good long time, neighbor. We got each other's backs. Not one without the other, neighbor. Not one without the other. And you're going to feel the pain, neighbor. Leo Action has you on the run. Each of us has his own God. And our God—mine and Leo's—is payback, revenge, eye for a motherfucking eye. You want a fair world, you got to make it, take it, fake it. You got to—"

Remmie blinked, scowled Trevor's voice from his head.

Stress, man.

Too little sleep.

He felt half-awake, like a creature from a horror film. Shit, Remmie, you need to rest. Next place to stop, you're going to...He spotted a well-constructed building a quarter mile off, west side of the highway. Damn it all to hell: It was a church. Catholic by the looks of the steeple, all ornate and self-righteous, like a flagpole with a hard-on for God.

He wanted to keep driving, to press on until he found a cantina, a family-run winery, a motor lodge with half-clean baños, but...He nodded off, jerked awake. Shit—if you sleep for a half-hour, you can drive for another two. Damn God all to hell, Remmie told himself, but you better take sanctuary when you see it. Isn't that the point of a church? Sanctuary?

Remmie turned into the church's gravel parking lot, slid to an abrupt stop.

Out front of the angular building, in a black get-up with a stiff, white collar, a Mexican priest stood with a copy of the Holy Bible hugged to his chest. It looked like he was waiting for somebody.

You, Remmie. Father here wants to have a chat with you.

You better wake the fuck up, Remmie.

God just talked back to you.

Finally.

● ● ●

The church smelled of day-old tortillas and oxidized red wine.

Remmie said to himself: The body and blood of Christ.

The priest, tall for a Mexican, wandered through the rows of wooden pews toward the altar. Above him, another crucifix glared at Remmie, but this one held a tortured Jesus leering like a prisoner. So fucking morbid, this whole Jesus-on-the-cross thing. The church itself was drab, a wooden building constructed without craft or artistry; Remmie imagined a loose affiliation of underpaid locals nailing two-by-fours together. He wondered how the steeple hard-on managed to stay upright.

Remmie followed the priest at a distance, his breath crushed into a ball inside his chest. What was he so nervous about? Wasn't this like walking into a fairy tale, a museum of myth? Maybe, but it scared him, too. All this talk of hell and purgatory and...Shit, who knew what the truth was anymore? Not Remmie. He figured, after the last two days, he didn't know shit about shit. Never would neither. Not if the world could help it.

The priest stopped at the altar, kneeled, crossed himself. He bowed his head for the appropriate duration and mumbled to himself. Afterwards he stood and faced Remmie, his flat, rounded features draped in shadow. "What brings you to the house of the Lord, señor...?"

"Miken. Mr. Remmie Miken. I come from—"

"Los Estados Unidos. I can see that." The priest folded his arms across the leather bible, waited.

Remmie scraped his feet against the polished cement floor, smoothed the front of his Hawaiian shirt. He was aware of the sound his hands made against the fabric, like sandpaper on skin. He said, "I just need to kill some time. That's about it. I need...I need some sleep, father."

The priest nodded. After a long, sobering silence, he pointed at a pew near the front of the church.

Remmie moved forward, sat where instructed.

"Lay down if you wish."

"I mean, I can just sit here for a little bit and pay my respects."

"And to who will you pay these respects?" The priest had perfect posture, almost like a steel spike ran down through him from heaven itself.

"God in heaven," Remmie said.

"And his only begotten son?"

"If you say so, padre. If it means I have to say so while I'm here."

The priest shrugged. "Respect what you will. Life, I hope." His round eyes narrowed, kept on Remmie's slumped frame. "At the very least."

"What's that mean?"

"You have blood on your hands, friend."

Remmie looked down at his hands—holy shit. His hands were caked in blood. Trevor's blood. From when he got shot. From when Remmie tried to...Why hadn't he washed? He didn't remember the blood being on his hands while he drove...But, yes, it was. And Gonzo not saying one word. Good riddance to that fucker. This was like running around with mayonnaise on your face. Holy shit, indeed. Remmie shoved his hands beneath his thighs, like a kid trying to keep himself from reaching for a candy bowl. "It's nothing, just a thing I had to do…" His voice trailed off. Remmie could think of nothing to say. He was in the bowels of a rural Catholic church with a dead man's juices running across his knuckles. That was the whole of it.

The priest said, "Are you baptized?"

"For what?"

"To cleanse the evil from your soul."

"Shit. My mom used to drag us down the street to an old Pentecostal, but I never had a holy man lay his hands on me. Nope, I don't believe I'm baptized. You think it'll make me feel different?" Remmie felt stupid for asking such a question.

Hawaiian shirt. Bloody knuckles. Stupid questions.

God, Remmie thought, I must need saving.

"What is it you've lost?"

This fucking priest and his questions.

Remmie said, "Came down here looking for a girl." He decided it was hard to lie with the dead Jesus staring at him.

"She's got some money. And a nice car."

"What kind of woman is she?"

"I can't say. I never met her. Only saw her in a picture."

"And you're afraid for her?"

"Maybe. I'm drawn toward her, whatever the hell that means."

"A divine attraction," the priest said. "Like a man is drawn to God."

"You said it. Not me."

"I have seen men drawn to everything in this world. I have seen men who cannot live without tequila, alcohol. Men who cannot live without machine guns, drugs, killing. Men who are slaves to the toil of the fields. Legal and otherwise. I have seen men drawn to far places, promises of money and security."

"Over the border."

"Es correcto. I have seen men who run from themselves. I think this is what you are."

Remmie grunted, tried hard not to laugh. All this religious booby-trap stuff made him feel funny. "Who says I'm not running after myself, headed right for myself?" Riddle me that, motherfucker.

The priest took his turn to laugh. It was a one note, abrupt sound, a laugh steeped in driven thought. The man who thinks too much laughs too little. "You have nothing behind you, señor Miken. Even the wind can see this, and so can God. I can tell you are nothing without the road. It's why you—"

"Went with him."

"That's right," the priest said. "Es correcto. And there is death behind you, too. But he doesn't need to follow, death. He waits for you instead."

"You saying I'm going to die?"

"I'm saying we all die." The priest smirked.

Remmie wondered if the man was fucking with him. "You're a real talky priest, but you don't say much of anything, do you?"

"I speak without talking, listen without hearing."

Jee-zus, Remmie thought. *Kee-rist.* "I'm too tired for spells and riddles, but I'll take a little holy water if you have it."

"We have Dasani, bottled water."

"It's not holy?"

"I can make the sign of the cross for you."

Remmie said, "And that will get it done?"

The priest stood. He adjusted his white collar, moved the bible from one arm to the other. "You can sleep here for two hours, but after that I must prepare a mass. Would you like a blanket?"

Remmie shrugged and said, "If it isn't too much trouble."

"Nothing is too much trouble for God."

Remmie remembered the blood on his hands. He thought: I hope like hell this tricky priest is right. The priest returned with the water and blanket and, before long, Remmie slept.

23

WHILE HE SLEPT, REMMIE SPOKE with Trevor Spends.

They sat in the diner. The same place from two days ago. And Trevor ate the eggs Benedict with a plump smile on his face, his cheeks moving like balloons as he chewed and talked. "You know, neighbor," he said, "I never understood what was so scary about death. Way I see it, you just wake up somewhere else. I mean, look, I know it doesn't always go down like that. There's people have a rougher time of it, this dying thing. But let's say, one day, you go to sleep all warm in your bed. And, shit, the big man up top calls your number, says it's lights out for you, time for the dirt nap? You just don't wake up, take your shower, your shit. And you don't spend ten hours flipping burgers or taking out the trash, right? Selling used cars, delivering junk mail, whatever it is you do. That's all in the past. And you wake up in this other place. What's so fucking bad about that?"

Remmie chewed pancakes and, from what he could tell,

they never ended. A skinny waitress poured them cheap bourbon straight from the bottle—syrup-thick and brown. "I guess it's just, you don't know what that place is, what's on the other side. Is it good? Bad? Is it hell? That's what gets people, I think. It's that they—"

"Oh, shit." With a crumpled napkin, Trevor dabbed at egg yolk on his tie. "My fucking dry-cleaning man is going to kill me." He finished dabbing, tossed the napkin onto the table, picked up his fork. He ate and talked. "What's on the other side? Okay, I guess you could get your panties in a bunch about all that, but—ooh, you know what? Let me tell you about this guy I knew. He's dead now, but he won't mind I tell you about him."

"The dead don't mind," Remmie said. He was thick into the bourbon. Fuck pancakes.

"No, they don't. Never saw a dead man couldn't take an insult. And I mean that." Trevor laughed until it filled the diner.

No matter. The two men were alone.

"Anyhow," Trevor said, "This guy I knew sat on the corner of Market and Forty-first, right outside the little corner store there. That's how I met him, coming out with a half-pint of Chivas. Anyway, turns out this guy, this cranky old bastard with red alkie eyes and a paunch like a basketball, has himself a Pee-H-Dee. I'm talking the real thing now. Not some internet thing you buy through PayPal. Like, you know how easy it is to become a preacher these days?"

"Fill out a form and send in the money."

"Yes, sir," Trevor said. "It's like buying a bus ticket. Here you go, pastor bumfuck of pay dirt church. But not this guy, okay? He's got the real thing, even has papers published in all these places and such. Nothing you'd read now. Not that kind of stuff. But what other people smarter than us two read."

117

"Nobody reads a goddamn one of them," Remmie said.

"He used spell check and everything."

"Might as well have made up his own fucking alphabet."

Trevor said, "This is beside my point. Now, I'm talking about this man, who he is..." Trevor stopped forking eggs into his mouth, planted both elbows on the table, waved the fork like a magic wand. "This guy practically studied the pimples on Shakespeare's fucking chin. He's a sonnet man, this son of a gun, and he knows a Shakespeare sonnet like an alley cat knows a dumpster. And what he wanted, he says to me, was a way to see the world as meaningful. Like, he was trying to figure out: Did it all—all this, you know—mean something besides... Besides whatever."

"Another seeker of truth, huh?"

"Less than that, neighbor. Meaning is all he wanted. And he gets all into these sonnets, goes on and gets himself a Pee-H-Dee, but he can't find a square foot of meaning, not for real anyhow. Nope—it's crickets in the old Pee-H-Dee head. Pure...empty...silence. So, you know what he does? Son of a gun goes and decides to wander around, just hit the streets. No money. No home. No fucking spare underwear. It's just Mr. Pee-H-Dee and a pair of Rite-Aid flip-flops. There he is, sitting outside a corner liquor store with a two-week beard and lips so chapped he could refurbish a porcelain tub with the suckers." Trevor shoved the last of his yolky eggs into his mouth, chewed hard and loud. "You got a story to match that?"

Remmie sat in the booth and groaned, grunted, coughed. He sipped from his mug of thick bourbon. Even in dreams, he thought, the world is goddamn senseless. Meaning? Fuck meaning.

This life is all breathing into the void, teetering on the lip of doom, steering around the steaming piles of shit.

He shook his head. "No, I don't have a story to match that. I can't say I ever will."

Trevor stopped chewing and an odd silence filled the diner. The big man leveled his eyes at Remmie and said, "Don't you worry, Remmie Miken. One day you will have a story to match that. I swear it. On my own double-wide and twice-deep grave. I swear it from here to hell and back again."

Remmie lifted his mug and drank.

24

WHEN HE AWOKE, REMMIE SMELLED the warm, lard-rich smell of tamales. He sat up and saw an old woman carrying a paper grocery sack. She was placing a tamale—wrapped in thin tinfoil—on each pew in spaces about a foot apart. She turned and narrowed her eyes at Remmie, decided he was okay. "¿Tienes hambre? You want it?" She patted her belly and reached into the paper sack, came out with a tamale and waved it at him.

Remmie liked his luck after the nap. Nothing like waking up and staring dinner in the face. How long did he sleep? Felt like a year, but maybe an hour. Less even. He stood and walked toward the woman. "Gracias, señora. I am so hungry. I haven't eaten since, hell..." Last night? Yes, at the restaurant. Before Trevor got lit up and—before Trevor took the dirt nap.

The woman waited for Remmie to reach her, handed him the greasy tamale and smiled.

The package was warm in his palm, like a river stone warmed over a campfire. Remmie bowed to the woman. This he did not understand; it simply happened.

The woman returned the bow and went to her work. Tamale here. Tamale there.

Some mass this would be...Remmie thought it made sense. Everybody likes a snack.

The devout more than most.

Outside, the moon hung half full and low over the distant hills. The Mustang was still there, but Remmie noted the rear spoiler—aftermarket, too—had been swiped. Choosy motherfucking thieves, weren't they? Some Mexican teenagers watching too many Hollywood rice burner movies. At least they left the car itself. Before he got into the car, Remmie placed the warm tamale on the roof, removed his Hawaiian shirt, shook it out in the cool wind. The air felt good on his skin, like he was walking through pool water at a fancy resort. Remmie shrugged the shirt back across his shoulders, grabbed his tamale and unwrapped it. The food was warm, moist, filled with spice and flavor. The inside was stuffed with pork and a white cheese Remmie loved. They sprinkled it over the taco salad at the restaurant where he worked. Shit. He thought of work. You wouldn't think it, but salad station was the worst gig in a restaurant. See, people expected salads to be ready fast, but they didn't see all the craftsmanship went into the damn thing; you have to layer one ingredient on top of the other. Not too much dressing. Not too little. Small amounts of tiny ingredients. Hell, when it came down to it the salad station was like surgery. You get good enough and you're the only one they want doing it on busy nights. Not Remmie. He knew that trap. Nothing he wanted to step into—Remmie stayed on fry duty, did it well enough to get by, but not well enough to move up. This was the story of every story in his fucking life.

And right here, down in paradise Mexico, leaning against a decent looking Mustang, tamale in hand and between his teeth, Remmie was suddenly fed up. It was the same feeling he had when he threw the dead pimp into the bay with Trevor, but a wee bit different. He was fed up, but he saw a way out beyond money. Like, added on with the money—Veranda Cline.

He thought about what he'd say when he met her for the first time.

"They call me Remmie."

Wait, is that your name? Or is that just what they call you?

"My name's Remmie Miken, Miss Cline. I'm here to save your ass."

Does this look like an ass that needs saving?

"Miss, every ass needs a little saving once in a while. Let me just—"

A lopsided mini pickup pulled into the parking lot. An old man hobbled out, half-waved to Remmie, entered the church. Another car pulled up, a late model Ford SUV. A family of four in their Sunday best exited, ignored Remmie. They too entered the church. Remmie chewed his tamale for the next ten minutes, watched families and old folks pull into the lot, lock their cars, amble into the church for mass. He knew, inside, they were munching on tamales like him. But he felt no kinship with the churchgoers. Remmie was confused. He stood in the cool wind. His shirt flapped and exposed the pale skin of his belly. He watched a bunch of Mexicans enter a church. Yes, he was confused. All over the world people were doing this very thing. Leaving their homes and wandering into churches. Every-damn-where, and he—Remmie Miken—was not a part of it. No, sir. He was a castaway, a throw-away, a no good...

Remmie crunched the greasy tinfoil into a ball, tossed it against the wind. It flew back at him, rolled along the dirt, stopped to rest near his boot. That fucking tinfoil looked just like Remmie felt: lost, alone, greasy, good for nothing. That, as sad as it was, did not confuse Remmie. That, he understood. He stepped on the tinfoil, crushed it flat.

I better get back on the road, he reminded himself, need to make Puerto Santo Thomás by sunrise.

• • •

Cool wind splashed Remmie in the face, whipped through his close-cropped hair. His shirt collar flapped wildly in the night. The Mustang ran throaty and hunched along the curved Mexican highway; the road tilted upward into scrublands and occasional villages perched between low lying valleys. Every once in a while, Remmie spotted a sign with a corporate name he recognized—fruit and vegetable companies burrowed into Me-hi-co like ticks. If you grow it, the workers will come.

Besides that, the road was empty.

It ran that way for twenty miles. And a lone black Mustang hurtled missile-like through the cool Mexican night. But Remmie ran into something he shouldn't have. Bad. Evil.

Hell in the night.

It happened when he came out of the hills, down along a flat stretch of highway. Ahead, boxy and gray in the distance, Remmie saw what he thought was the winery Gonzo mentioned. The landmark for Remmie to head west, toward the Pacific. He slowed the Mustang, watched for a dirt road. There were other buildings along the highway, ramshackle structures of adobe and cinder-brick; Remmie spotted a church building, a school with an old play set rusting in a dirt lot. He saw a general store and a tire shop. These, he knew, were the markings of another Mexican town nestled in the hills. Another rundown deletion on the Mexican map.

He reached a trio of houses with corrugated metal roofs, chicken coops visible out front beside well-used pickup trucks. There, dark and twisting and dusty, a dirt road emerged. Remmie swung the Mustang westward, slid in loose gravel, regained control and zoomed beneath an odd assortment of eucalyptus trees reaching straight and tall toward the night sky. He felt as if he was driving through a haunted forest.

And then the spotlight swept him.

A blinding light through the windshield. So hot it burned his forehead.

Gunfire came next. The tap-tap-tap of a semi-automatic machine gun raising its voice—warning shots. Remmie slowed the Mustang, stopped. He kept the engine running, waited until he saw two silhouettes drift out of the spotlight, alien beings in his windshield. No, not aliens at all. They were men. One, a squat figure with burly arms and a pistol tapping against his thigh. The other, a taller string bean body type with a long gun, likely the machine gun. With the light in his eyes, Remmie couldn't tell for certain.

He heard the Spanish command to open his door. Remmie hesitated. He did think about the empty pistol beneath his seat, but pulling that would get him killed for real, like what happened with Trevor. Big time dead in little Mexico. The silhouettes moved to each side of the Mustang. Floor it then? Plow through these fuckers and try to...No, Remmie wasn't going anywhere. An engine sound burned through the air. Shapes appeared through the windshield. Pickup trucks on fat toothy tires. Roll cages. The vehicles—three of them—crossed in front of the spotlight, stopped, waited. More men; men driving and riding shotgun and men in the beds of the pickups. What was this? Again, the command to open his door. A demand. A promise of violence.

Remmie did as he was told.

He placed one foot in the dirt, unfolded himself from the Mustang. He stood there grunting and squinting, tried hard to count the guns pointed at him.

"What's your name, gringo?" Big Arms asked.

"My name's Remmie. I'm trying to get to—"

"Paradise," Big Arms said. "We know. Everybody with white skin is trying to get to paradise." He moved toward Remmie, motioned with the pistol: *Come here, gringo.*

Remmie cleared his throat, sniffed hard until he felt the cold air cleanse his throat, give him a voice behind all his fear and ass-clenching. "What are you—"

Big Arms lashed out with the pistol, a snake striking in the dark. The butt of the gun knocked hard into Remmie's nose, sent a flare of pain through his jaw and into the center of his forehead. He coughed twice and groaned, sank to his knees.

"I didn't see a goddamn thing. The fuck are you—"

The next blow landed on the back of Remmie's neck. He felt it run all the way down to the tip of his dick. His entire body throbbed. He toppled into the dirt, somehow pulled himself back from the ironclad certainty of unconsciousness. The road smelled like artichoke and sage. Beer bottle caps were sprinkled everywhere. He looked up at the squat silhouette and said, "I don't know what's happening to me, why I'm here in the…"

Big Arms squatted next to Remmie. "You came to paradise for poquito dinero, no? Isn't that what it is? Oh, and a girl, no?"

Remmie didn't speak. Couldn't speak.

He imagined himself swimming through the syrup-like

bourbon from his Trevor dream.

"You thinking maybe you want to lie, huh? Give a men-tira, no? That you?"

Remmie tried to shake his head, but knew the motion wasn't visible. He tasted dirt.

Big Arms tapped Remmie's head with the butt of his pistol, used a taco-smelling hand to twist Remmie's head to one side. "Look it, gringo," he said. "I got something good for you, an old friend of yours. ¿Tu amigo, no?"

Remmie struggled to open his eyes. He fought back nausea. From the yellow spotlight's endless depths came another silhouette. It staggered, grunted, fell in the dirt beside Remmie.

The silhouette cleared, came into focus.

Gonzo.

And he was bleeding.

• • •

Remmie awoke with a burlap sack over his head—you say potato, and I say a big fucking sack over your head. They were moving, and he felt the wind passing through the sack, smacking him in the face like dry ice. He braced himself against steel and flesh. He thought, I'm riding in back of one of the pickup trucks. A lumpy body slumped beside him. Gonzo? Remmie heard a grunt. Deep voices shouted through the wind. The road became rutted and their speed slowed. He noted a tilt upwards, sharp curves, the texture of gravel and dried mud.

His head ached like hell. Pins jabbed into his forehead. A burn floated down the back of his head, into his spine. He wanted to vomit, held it back, breathed heavy through the burlap and thick scent of root vegetables.

After another twenty minutes thundering around hairpin

curves, the truck slid to a stop. A cacophonous chorus of engines sputtered, died. Men's voices prowled the night in thick-tongued Spanish. Remmie shifted, tried to lift the sack with tied hands. A fist crashed into his neck.

The same vomit pang tore through his belly. "The fuck is this? Let me out—"

"Silencio, gringo. This is not your country. You are far from home."

Remmie struggled as hands gripped his shoulders, yanked him from the pickup. He spilled onto muddy soil. He pressed into the mud with his hands, tried to stand and run. But another pair of hands gripped him, shoved hard. Remmie stopped struggling.

He waited. Boot crunching sounds surrounded him, settled into silence. Another body fell into the mud, rolled once. The body groaned; it was near Remmie and he tried to reach out, grasped only mud. A man laughed somewhere.

A gun magazine slammed into its slot.

Big Arms said, "We going to tell you only this one time, gringo. Leo Action comes down into Baja, he gets somebody killed. He's a puto, sabes? Motherfucker. And if we have to, if we want to, we going to go and fuck his mother. But first, we have to fuck his men. Like gordo here."

Remmie spoke through the sack, "I'm not with Leo Action. Neither is this son of a—"

A boot sole in Remmie's throat cut him off. He gagged, wretched.

"No more sending money down into Baja. It comes," Big Arms said, "and we going to take it like the men we are. Sabes? No more drugs from Baja for Leo Action. He wants it, he has to buy from us. But too bad, we going to sell in his neighborhood now. No reason for him to buy it, he can't sell it. I'm trying to tell you, gringo—your boss is not welcome in

Baja. No more Action in Baja. But just to make sure, we have to send a message."

Remmie heard groans beside him, frantic breaths. It must be Gonzo there in the mud. Who else could it be? And these men had him and Gonzo confused with Leo Action's men; Remmie didn't know what to do. Send a message? The fuck did that mean? Through the burlap, he said, "I'm telling you, you got the wrong fucking people, man. I'm just down here trying to find a girl for a friend. I'm just—" Gunfire stopped him mid-sentence. Again, the three staccato coughs; laughing started among the men who surrounded Remmie and Gonzo.

Big Arms said, "Está bien."

And then rushed, hacking gunfire. Grunting agony from the man beside Remmie, the two of them stationary targets in the mud. Harsh cries now, a throbbing scream that echoed through the gag in Gonzo's mouth.

More gunfire, the oomph-oomph-oomph of bullets striking flesh.

"Jesus, man!" Remmie screamed. "I didn't do shit to you!"

And, again, more gunfire silenced him. Beside Remmie, Gonzo trembled, shook.

Laughter from the men, a percolating, hyena-like laughter. Remmie knew that laughter, its origin—that laughter was madness. Nothing else. Pure madness. And since the moment when Remmie knocked on that tenement door and Trevor Spends answered, he had encountered nothing but madness; this, then—pure and utter madness—had become his life. The priest's face and voice came to his mind for some reason. He saw those hard features ceaselessly speaking of God. But in the priest's eyes, he saw nothing. Vacancy. And that, too, was a madness.

Remmie wanted to scream: Please, please don't kill me.

I've done nothing. In my life, I mean, I've done nothing. My whole life has been an endless punching of the time clock. Don't kill me here, not now, when I'm so close to, to, to Veranda! To the love that awaits me here in paradise! No, don't kill me, don't, don't, don't…

And the engines started again. Their mechanical grunts and coughs filtered through the burlap into Remmie's ears.

A hand ripped at his head, yanked the sack off him. Big Arms leaned into the wash of headlights, centered a lopsided grin on Remmie. "Have a nice trip home, gringo. May God let us never see you again here in Baja. A little prayer for you, huh?"

And the headlights swam at Remmie, circled him. Big Arms vanished. The pickup trucks circled again, like sharks. Their exhaust pipes spit at him like the nostrils of some giant creature. And then they spun and spat around a hairpin curve in the road. The engine noise faded.

Remmie tried to slow his breathing. He lay there in the mud, let his eyes adjust to the now-complete darkness. He saw Gonzo's body beside him. It was covered in a sheet soaked by blood. Brown-black mud ran up the sheet's sides, mixed with the blood to form a dark smear against the body. The figure was motionless—dead.

Remmie rolled onto his back.

As he stared at the hot stars in the cool blue sky, Remmie considered prayer.

But he didn't pray. Instead, he closed his eyes and slept.

25

THE SUNLIGHT HIT REMMIE'S FACE and he opened his eyes. A crow was perched on Gonzo's body, staring with the black-eyed gaze of death. An after-omen. Remmie raised a hand and the crow took flight, circled high into the blue sky. Remmie watched until he felt his eyes crossing, blinked hard and pulled himself into a sitting position. In his midsection, a twinge of sharp pain struck, washed through him in a slow, warm wave—a couple ribs, maybe broken. Cracked, if he was lucky. From when they tossed him out of the truck.

And, yes, Remmie was lucky. He was nothing if not that.

Lucky as a whore on a misty Friday night. The bad kind of lucky.

His head ached, and his throat was swollen. Woe is me, Remmie thought, and then he put it out of his mind. What was it his uncle used to say?

Oh, Forget it. Hell, you can't remember anyhow.

Remmie scanned his surroundings. He was on a plateau.

It looked down on a valley. Straight-line crops in dull squares and the hillsides overgrown with brush. A small, disheveled town to the south. He spotted the dirt road where he'd turned the night before and, following that line, saw the Mustang. He could see, even from that height, the car was worth nothing. They'd lit it on fire. The stealthy, once-black body looked gray and dry. Brittle like the cracked shell of a summer beetle. This didn't surprise Remmie.

In fact, he didn't much care. Except that now he had to walk.

He turned his attention to Gonzo.

Damp blood coated half the sheet, clung to the body like wet tissue paper. Gonzo's legs were spread oddly in the drying mud. A lone hand—motionless, pale—jutted palm up from beneath Gonzo's beer belly. Remmie noted coin-sized callouses. Gonzo's thick black curls spilled over his face. Yes, he was dead. And it wasn't pretty.

Remmie wiped Gonzo's curls back over his forehead, met the gaze of a lone, matted eye, big as a testicle. Gonzo's nose rested in the mud—talk about brown-nosing.

Remmie said, "Bet you didn't expect this shit."

There was no reply.

Remmie grunted and struggled to his feet. He felt unsteady, crushed up against himself, as if he'd been pulled through a collapsing tunnel. From what he felt, though, Remmie thought it would all be aches and pains—nothing that lasted. He took one last look at Gonzo, moved his lips as if to pray, but said nothing. Another hombre taking the dirt nap, or so they say.

Remmie turned from the body and began to stagger. After a few strides, he had his feet beneath him. He rounded a hairpin curve in the dirt road, and the valley shrank from view. What about the body? It would rot up here, melt into teeth and bones. What else could he do?

Nothing, like always. Like it had been forever. Remmie could do nothing.

He traversed a narrow canyon and noticed trash scattered below him. Aluminum cans and junk food wrappers. Plastic shopping bags torn to shreds. Water trickled through the gulley and, for a moment, Remmie considered climbing down for a drink. He decided against it; no use wetting your whistle just to breathe fire from your ass. That sounded like something his uncle would have said. But no, Remmie reflected, I'm the one saying it. He walked for a half mile before the sun started to get to him. Remmie thought it must be close to 100 degrees. Sweat ran across his chest, coated the muddied and torn Hawaiian shirt. He unbuttoned the shirt, let it trail out behind him. His pants became wet with sweat. His lips were already cracked from sleeping and, after walking another mile, they felt like they'd been peppered with shrapnel.

Remmie kept walking.

The road curved snake-like through scrubland hills. It wasn't that the land was barren, but that it was desolate. It was tough. Hard. Mean.

Remmie understood this, knew the one bit of grace was the nearby ocean pushing moisture into the valleys—this was how things grew.

Another hot mile. And another. The dust kicked up beneath Remmie's boots and he sneezed uncontrollably for a minute or so. He wiped his mouth with the dirty underside of his wrist and, still, kept walking. Where was he going? Down from this fuck-stick mountain, that's where. Down through the flat, segregated crops of brussels sprouts and cabbage and poor-sweet strawberries. He was headed—yes, still...because why not?—for Puerto Santo Thomás.

For the money.

For Veranda Cline.

Her face still burned in his head, an etched image loading across misfiring synapses. He followed the image, blinked away his endless flowing sweat and tears.

After an hour walking, he descended into a wider canyon shaded by Eucalyptus trees. The temperature dropped and Remmie felt himself breathe easier. A bit farther into the shade, past a pickup truck with flat tires and a missing door, Remmie saw a building. It was a cinder-brick dwelling surrounded by cholla. Two windows without glass stared at him like cartoon eyes. The wooden door between them was a nose. Remmie noticed the yard was well-kept, raked recently, and with a uniform set of garbage bins on one side. It might be the home of a farmer, or someone who worked on a nearby farm and never—like most—made much, if any, money.

This was a poor man's house.

But Remmie knew that poor men, too, drank water.

Other thoughts did cross Remmie's mind. But what he thought about most was water.

Cold, clear water. The gosh darn liquid of life.

He gulped and shuffled toward the door.

He noticed an etching in the door's center, about eyeball height. Another fucking crucifix. If Remmie wasn't sick of God by the time he escaped Mexico, he figured he'd turn himself over to Catholicism. *Why not, if you can bear it for this long?*

He cleared his throat of both God and phlegm.

Remmie considered: Should he call out? Rap twice on the door? Kick the damn thing in and take whatever he wanted? He had nothing to trade, and his wallet and money were gone, taken by Gonzo's wild-eyed killers.

Lucky for Remmie—there's that whore's luck again—he didn't have to make a decision.

The unmistakable click-clunk sound of a lever action rifle made the decision for him.

26

THE OLD MAN'S RIFLE POKED REMMIE like a lizard's pecker. Remmie was face down in the dirt. Again. He breathed in the smell of foot-packed earth and years of neglect; from the looks of the old man, he lived alone. Remmie waited while he poked and prodded, dragged the rifle barrel from the nape of Remmie's neck down to his asshole, gave a little push and hooted laughter.

After he stopped laughing, the old man said, "Bien."

Remmie stood, didn't bother to brush the dirt from his chest and thighs.

The old man had two teeth, both off-center in the top ridge of his mouth; one tooth—the bigger of the two—was black with rot. He had a nice smile and was willing to use it. He was short and skinny, tan as belt leather from his forehead to where his scrawny neck disappeared below a frayed LA Dodgers t-shirt. He wore baggy beige pants and tan work boots. His hands were hard knots of callous and muscle—his body and posture were those of a working man. He blinked rarely and kept his eyes on Remmie. They stood in silence until the man hooted laughter again, slung the rifle across one shoulder. His smile became a grin.

Remmie got right to it. "¿Agua, señor? ¿Agua?" He tapped his lips with a finger, rubbed his throat. He was surprised at the bird-like sound of his voice.

The old man turned and led Remmie into the house. It was dark inside except for the sun coming through the two window openings. Flies buzzed around Remmie's head. The old man had a tattered couch in one corner, a shelf of paperback books next to it, and a big red bucket of the sort you get from a hardware or large retail store. The old man leaned the rifle against the wall near the couch, reached into the bucket—Remmie heard the jumble of ice cubes—and yanked out two bottles of Modelo beer. He smiled again and handed Remmie a bottle after popping both caps with the silver wedding band on his finger.

Remmie took the beer, gulped down a bit, wiped his lips with the back of a hand. The beer was good, but he still wanted water. He walked to the bucket, got down on his hands and knees, and plunged his face into the ice-cold bucket. His cheeks and lips burned with cold. The ice was part melted and Remmie had to drink slowly around the floating beer bottles and slippery cubes. It felt good going down, like cold spring water tinged with the flavor of beer— not a bad combination.

When he was finished, Remmie pulled out of the bucket and sat cross-legged on the cement floor, his back against the wall. He cradled the beer in his lap, sipped from it with caution. Getting too drunk would not do him well at the moment...Who knew what this old man was up to? After the previous night, Remmie found himself wary of Mexicans.

The old man sat on the couch and gulped from his beer. He pointed a wobbly finger at Remmie and said, "¿Viajes, eh? ¿Esta bien, no?"

"Bad travels. Mexico is mean." Remmie rubbed at his ribs, tried to make some sort of facial expression to convey his pain.

The old man nodded and, after thinking some, said, "Comprendo." In partial English, he added: "Mexico, es... Hurt me." He pointed the wobbly finger at his heart.

Remmie said, "Trabaja, right? A lot of work? Too much work?"

The old man shrugged, hooted laughter. "Yes, work! Too much!" His body shook and he coughed, washed it down with beer. He stood and grabbed another bottle, waited for Remmie to request another round, shrugged and sat down when he didn't.

"Cual es..." Remmie made a digging motion with his arms.

The old man said, "Fresas."

Strawberries—not a surprise to Remmie, and a handful of strawberries sounded good. Damn good. "You have some? ¿Tiene fresas?"

The old man stood, wandered into a back room and reappeared with a paper plate. He handed it to Remmie. Six strawberries of varying sizes. White mold clung to their undersides. He figured these for the cast offs, what they sent home with the workers. He bit the topsides from two of the berries, tasted half-bitter flesh in his mouth. Not like a kiss. More like a punch. He set the plate on the cement, nodded a thanks.

The old man said, "¿No bueno, eh?" Again, the hooting and rambunctious laughter.

A joke then. Remmie finished his beer. The old man

nodded, stood and handed Remmie a new opened bottle. They drank. Both men smiled at each other. This went on for about an hour. Remmie felt himself getting drunk—so much for sober. It seemed the bucket was endless in its supply of cerveza, and the old man was all too willing to share. Every few minutes, the old man would grunt or laugh and say, "¿Bueno, eh? ¿Es bueno?"

Remmie nodded affirmation. It was good, wasn't it?

Remmie was deep into his fifth or sixth beer when he heard the roar of an engine.

The old man smiled big with his two front teeth and said, "Mi amigo. Es bueno." He stood and lifted the rifle, drained the last of his beer and tossed the bottle into the bucket. With the rifle, he walked into the yard.

Remmie stood and followed.

● ● ●

A white man hopped out of the Volkswagen Bug, unfolded like a slinky from the small yellow car, its curved and insect-like frame edged by a steel cage. Remmie remembered they used those things down here for a big race, the Baja 1000, but he couldn't recall seeing this model of car modified for rough driving. He liked the car's look and sound. The driver stood a head taller than Remmie; he wore a gray-black beard down to a point in the center of his chest. His eyes, too, were gray in their deep sockets, and he was shirtless. His frame, though old—he might be fifty, sixty, or seventy—was lithe with long muscle and the hard look of a lifetime of work. You didn't look like this guy after watching thirty years of reality tv. This son of a gun meant business. The old man high-stepped toward the newcomer, hugged him with passion and joy. Remmie watched the two embrace. He wobbled a bit with his buzz. Must be the heat out here, he thought.

The old man rattled off Spanish, more stuff Remmie couldn't catch. Or throw.

The newcomer came around the car and shook both of Remmie's hands. Hell, the man shook Remmie's very soul. "How the fuck you doing, pal? Not often I see a fellow gringo in these hills. Hell, I don't rarely see a white rabbit, even when I go the old," he pointed to the center of his head, "mojo to my brain path. Drugs, man. I like 'em. Hell, brother man. I fucking love 'em. You know how it is, you get old and the drug thing don't seem so stupid. Tell you what, brother man, I'm right about that. Mexicans over this way call me Flaco. Because I got a gut problem and can't gain no weight, no matter how many tacos I eat."

The old man moved beside Flaco and hooted his pleasant laughter. He planted the rifle in the dirt, leaned on it like a miscreant soldier.

Flaco smelled like lard and margarita mix, a bit of wet earth beneath all that. But he had an ocean air about him too, as if he'd just swam into shore after riding a wave. Maybe it was his long white hair, or the sun wrinkles that ran across his forehead and cheeks. Or his big white teeth framed by thin lips. Flaco said, "I live over that way a few clicks, out where you can see the big blue. I got whales in my window like it's a fucking cartoon. Not like old Rio here." Flaco slapped the old man on the shoulder. "He's got a cinder-brick shit palace. Good thing it's only seasonal, the man's summer home. While he tends to the most precious of berries."

The old man laughed at this, almost fell over laughing. He pointed at Flaco and looked at Remmie, "Flaco. Skinny bastard. You get it?"

Remmie got it, but he was surprised to learn the old man's name—Rio, or River. He said, "I got left for dead up there on—"

"Oh, yes you did," Flaco said. "I heard the trucks, knew it was that drug business again. They like to do their business out where nobody can see. Can't say I blame 'em, the way they have to carry on to keep all these poor fucks in line. Chain of command, brother man—it's the only thing keeps a walking boss sane."

Remmie said, "I'm not involved with drugs."

"Oh, come on now. All us motherfuckers are involved with drugs. No way around that." Flaco nodded at Rio. He said, "You mind I get a cold cerveza, amigo?"

Rio went into the house to get some beer.

Flaco draped his long thumbs in the waistband of his purple board shorts. "Thing of it is, they got the whole drug thing going personal now. You can't sling a little weed without getting your noggin knocked off. They'll cut your tongue out with the ripped edge of a fucking matchbook. You play around too much,you'll get yourself a free tour of the afterlife. How's that for rhetoric? Whatever it takes. I can't say they aren't persuasive. Me, I get my drugs from a guy I know around Mexicali. Don't ask me his name, fucker won't even tell me. And I spend enough to 1099 his ass. What about you? What are your dealings with the devil?"

Rio came out with three cold, open beers and the three of them drank.

After he chirped his wet lips, Remmie said, "Not a fucking thing. I got picked up last night and next thing I know, I'm breathing dirt."

"They burned up that car of yours." Fact, plain as heat on the wind.

"I guess so."

Flaco ducked his head to one side, finished his beer in a long, throat-shaking chug. "They burn up your car and beat your ass to hell, you got dealings with the men—it don't take the FBI to tell you that." He smiled at Remmie and lifted a blonde-tinged eyebrow. "Thing of it is, they let you go. What's that mean?" He reached for Rio's beer, took it, drank. After a second sip, he handed the bottle back to the old man. "Means they either want you to deliver a message, some kind that's more important than killing your ass. Or, way I see it, they want you to take them to something. Can't see how it goes another way."

"You mean, they want to follow me?"

"Did you play a detective on daytime tv? Damn, boy, you're smart."

The image of Veranda passed through Remmie's mind again. Then he remembered what Big Arms said. They wanted Remmie to deliver a message to Leo Action, but he didn't know how the hell to find the man. And he sure wasn't going to find out. Fuck. That. "I got nothing they need," he said.

"My papa used to say, 'You can want in one hand and shit in another, see which comes first. Let me tell you, these bastards shit and piss in whatever hands they want. You watch out or they're going to rip off your head and shit down your neck."

This was rough language, even for a trashy character like Remmie. He said, "Where'd you learn to hold a conversation, fucking military school?"

"That, and a little bar in Durham, North Carolina. Classy place out in the country. I take real pride in my presumptuous vocabulary."

Remmie said, "You got a way with words."

"Fucking-A, amigo." Flaco hitched up his shorts, scratched his chest with dirty fingernails. "Truth is, I don't trust a man who can't see it in himself to curse. Knew a guy once who promised he'd never so much as fucked a sentence with the word of shit. Guy never drank either; he called himself a tea-total-her. Actually used that word and wouldn't say fuck if it was the answer to a game of Hangman. You believe that? Anyhow, point to this little ditty is that the fucker went crazy. Shit, one day I wake up and open the newspaper, guess who went ahead and played pin the steak knife in the old wife? Mr. Murder himself—man wouldn't curse a storm, but he'd kill when it came down to it. He's got a nice studio up north, place they call Folsom. Might have heard a song or two about it." Flaco slapped Rio on the back and said, "Go ahead and give us a fuck you, amigo. We want to hear it."

The old man shook his head, tried to suppress a grin. "Fuck you," he said.

"Dang right. Fuck. You."

Remmie wondered what the hell this was all about. Here he was, caught in a conversation with a mad man and a Mexican berry farmer. He went ahead and said, "Fuck you."

"That's it," Flaco said. "Now, we're starting to get acquainted. Me and Rio here, we been drinking cervezas together since, hell, oh-eight or nine. Back when Los Estados Unidos kicked the ass of the working man. I had me a tract home in Vegas, thought I'd make a penny. Ran a Jeep tour business with an ex-con from Roanoke, V-A. Guy had a temper, but he knew how to cook the books and make the tax man miss...They went ahead and got us though, didn't they? Fuck, shit, and damn it all to hell. After that, I said, It's the Baja life for me, the Baja life for me..." He sang loud into the hot afternoon.

Rio mimicked him and did a three-step dance, "The Baja life for me!" He'd left his rifle in the house.

Remmie shifted, ran his tongue over chapped lips. "Where'd you say you live?"

Flaco raised his eyebrows, clapped his hands together

twice. A barely visible layer of dust erupted from them. He said, "Shit, didn't I say? I live over near Puerto Santo Thomás, where I can watch the whales fuck with a glass of red wine in my hand. You want to go and see my base camp? Hell, I got a spare room—I bet you're already sick of this cinder-brick shit palace."

Remmie didn't know what to say, but he sensed his jaw was hanging, adrift from his face.

"That's a little fishing village now, Puerto Santo Thomás."

"I know what it is."

Rio said, "La Mar."

"El Mar," Remmie corrected him.

"Not when you love it like we do," Flaco said. He ran a hand through his blonde-white hair, blew a puff of air from between his lips. "We call it La Mar, and we make sure to kiss it goodnight."

• • •

Flaco piloted the Volkswagen as if he was headed straight through a storm of asteroids. He kept both hands tight on the wheel, hunched forward, and clenched his eyes on the dirt road. His elbows flared outward as if ready to punish a seven-footer after a vicious battle for a rebound. That blonde-white hair, long and feathery, whipped atop his head. He kept the windows open and it was all Remmie could do to keep from retching. His ribs already pained him, but the dust filled his chest and throat with phlegm. Flaco yelled at him the entire time, didn't wait for a reply as they spun around corners in quick descent.

"What I learned about these drug guys is they understand respect. That's the only thing they care about, that and money. Oh. hell, you can bet they want lots of money, the kind you write home to mom about, brother-man. And if you disrespect them, if you so much as look at them wrong, you got a date with the reaper. The question is this: What the fuck are you taking them to?"

Remmie couldn't see how Veranda Cline interested the drug traffickers; what could they want with her? He decided to come clean, see what Flaco had to say about it. "I came down here with another guy, an associate of mine. We're after a girl, and a car she stole."

"And?" Flaco tore his eyes from the road and glared at Remmie.

Remmie gripped the lap belt with both hands. The Baja Bug screamed and rattled across the washboard road surface. "And some money...Maybe." He wasn't sure about the money. His bet was Veranda either hid it or spent it. What else do you do with money?

"Right," Flaco yelled through dust and the grunt-squeak of over-stressed European-made suspension components. "It's the money then. I'm telling you, these fuckers like money. Hell, they love money. They'd marry money if they could. 'Til death do ye motherfuckers part."

The road curled left in a hairpin shift. Flaco spun the wheel, punched hard on the gas. The Volkswagen felt as if it was sliding out from beneath Remmie. He screamed in a girlish tone, tried hard to grab at the flat dashboard, but found no purchase. The Manzanita and scattered Eucalyptus spun past him in green-brown collage—Remmie saw the dirty white goat before Flaco did, a brown-white flash in the yellow sun. He shouted an unintelligible mash-up between stop and no and goat, but it was too late.

And Flaco knew it was too late; he didn't slow or try to stop before he plunged into the goat.

Flaco punched hard on the accelerator.

• • •

The smack of flesh against steel is a sound Remmie never forgot. It made him think of spoons slapping turkey, but multiplied ten thousand times, and with a sickening scream for background. He figured the goat died on impact. Blood—more black than red—coated the windshield and hood. He swore a leg toppled over them, landed in the road.

Did the goat disintegrate?

Flaco, his biceps shuddering as the car slowed, grimaced in disappointment. "Ah, hell—I just killed about three thousand tacos."

"They have goat tacos?" Stunned, Remmie imagined a goat finding out he was to be slaughtered for distribution at a taco stand—disappointment knows no bounds.

Flaco slammed on the brakes and the car slid, stopped. They sat in the throaty wheeze of the engine, evening sun filtering through the scattered eucalyptus. "You want tacos? They gato tacos." Flaco guffawed at the joke, had a hard time removing his seatbelt. "Perro, too," He said. "But, shit—I killed some poor sucker's goat."

They got out of the car and surveyed the hit-and-stay scene.

A black smear ran bulbous across the sandy road. It looked to Remmie like a car dropped an oil pan, blew a thick seal. But it was clearly wet and thin as blood. Off to one side, in a clump of ankle high desert grass, the largest portion of the goat's body lay motionless. Scattered a few yards farther, in the center of the road, were two clumps that Remmie thought might be severed legs.

Flaco grunted, spit, dug a thick finger into one nostril. "Every time I kill a goat, a fascist gets his weeny dinged." He pulled something from his nose, flicked it at the goat's still carcass.

"A fascist gets what?"

"Punched in the dick."

Remmie did not know how to continue the conversation. Instead, he said, "I guess we better bury the fucker."

"Nonsense. The scavengers will do as their creator has endowed them."

Remmie walked nearer to the goat, bent to one knee. He reached out and put a shaking hand on the animal's bloody neck. He jumped back when the eyelids popped open and two bright black eyes shone like charcoal. "Shit, how the fuck?" He stumbled, caught himself, scrambled to his feet. "It's still alive. The fucking goat is alive."

"Great God almighty, you don't say?" Flaco stood there with his hands on his hips. After some thought, he used one long finger to scratch his chin. "I guess I better kill it then." He started back toward the Baja Bug.

"Wait," Remmie said. "How can you kill it?"

"With a bullet," Flaco said over his shoulder. He reached the car and started digging around on the floor, his lean frame stretched across the driver's seat. "I have a pistol in here somewhere."

"But it survived. We can't kill it, can we?"

"Can't? Shoot, we have to kill it." Flaco was walking back toward Remmie with a toy-like silver pistol in one hand. "Won this a few weeks ago in an Ensenada poker game. Came with the bullets and everything."

"Stop, Flaco." Remmie held out his hands to stop the skinny white man.

Both men watched the other.

Flaco said, "What are you, a goat fucker?"

"I just think he deserves to die...On his own terms. Don't we all deserve that?"

"He got impaled by a European compact car. That goat is

145

finished; all that's left is to put him all the way under. Otherwise, it's just torture."

"Don't you have respect for life?"

Flaco waved the gun above his head. "That's what this is, my lead respect."

"I think we should let him die with some fucking…" Remmie couldn't think of the word, but it was on the tip of his tongue. "Whatever the hell people want to die with."

"A goat isn't people, brother-man. A goat is just—"

"A goat has a soul!" Was that the Holy Spirit? No, just Remmie's newfound passion for the blood of life. He wondered how he'd gone so long without it. "A goat has a soul, and that soul is still inside that…" He pointed at the soon-to-be carcass. "Body!"

"The hell it is." Flaco brought the gun down, pointed it past Remmie at the goat.

"Oh, no you better not." Remmie moved in front of the goat, felt the burn of the pistol's gaze—though it was tiny—punch through him like an ulcer.

"What the hell are you doing? This is a real fucking gun. It'll hurt if I shoot you."

"I'm making a goddamn stand."

Flaco said, "In front of a dead goat?"

"He's not dead."

"He will be in about a fraction of a second."

"Don't, Flaco." Remmie moved to block the skinny, loco gringo as he came toward the goat.

"I'll shoot him dead!"

"Dammit, what the hell are you—"

A rifle round whistled past them, plunged into the Baja Bug, struck just below the driver's side door. Both Flaco and Remmie turned in surprise.

Coming down the dirt road, hitching back and forth atop

a tired-looking burro, a Mexican man in a straw hat levered the action on a rifle. Remmie's eyes caught the glinting sun as it flashed on the expelled rifle cartridge. The man screamed at them in animal-like hoots. He fired the rifle again and a round smacked the trees behind them. Remmie and Flaco hit the dirt.

Flaco tried to yell at the man, but another rifle round cut him off, smacked the dirt beside Remmie. Maybe this was it, Remmie's last breath. And it would come at the hands of a goat farmer. He'd die beside the half-shredded remains of a still soul-laden goat. These thoughts saddened him.

The heavy footsteps of the burro sounded nearby; the Mexican levered the rifle again.

He fired.

Beside Remmie and Flaco, the goat whimpered as the round struck him. After, he lay silent.

The man atop the burro said, "Muerte, ay..." And then he said, "Pinche gringos."

27

WHEN THEY REACHED FLACO'S HOUSE, Remmie stood outside in the dusty driveway and stared for a long few minutes at the rippling tongue that was the Pacific Ocean. Up here, a hundred feet above the seashore, the wind blew hard and flat, like a powerful air conditioner in a decent department store—Remmie scratched his red cheeks, tried not to aggravate his throbbing abdomen.

When they arrived, Flaco loped inside without inviting Remmie. Both men were distraught about the goat. Flaco, because the goat farmer called them gringos. And in that context, he said, it sure as hell wasn't a compliment. Remmie, because the goat got caught between accident and murder. It didn't seem fair. But then he thought: *maybe that's where I am, too.*

Maybe Remmie was caught down here in Baja, halfway between accident and murder. An accident to walk over and meet Trevor Spends, to help him chop up the pimp, give chase to Veranda. Murder...There was Trevor and Gonzo and—he hoped not Veranda. Or, hell, not him. If running into the cartel men taught Remmie anything, it was that death is ugly; death is a face plant in a mud hole. Usually, Remmie knew, it took war to teach a man things like that.

But Remmie got his lessons about death down here in Baja.

He blinked away dust, smirked at the swaying sea, and walked toward Flaco's front door.

● ● ●

Flaco lived in a mission-style house with an open floor plan. Red Mexican tile ran wall to wall and two bedrooms, each with a bathroom, flanked out in opposite directions, their entrances covered with Mayan-style blankets rather than doors. Bookshelves ran along each wall, nearly as high as the stucco ceiling. Remmie glanced at some titles as he walked in—there were rows and rows of magazines: *National Geographic, Playboy, Cosmopolitan, True West.* Along the far wall, he noticed thicker bindings. Row upon row of books. Trade paperbacks. Flaco sat in a leather couch in the center of the room. Opposite the couch was another couch, tan in color and of lesser quality. Between the couches was a low table with an unsolved jigsaw puzzle sitting on it. Remmie sat down in the tan couch and watched Flaco pour him a shot glass full with tequila.

Remmie said, "I guess you like to read, huh?"

"No, not really. This is all from the previous owner. Guy I knew from Taos, New Mexico. He ran a string of dry-cleaning shops out that way. You'd never know the money in a racket like dry cleaning. Plus, they get to keep all the money they find in the clothes. Not like the owners know they left money in a tweed blazer, am I right? He sold this place after they got caught laundering money for a snide fucker named Luca Manser, a local weapons guy. You know the type."

Remmie nodded, though he knew nothing of the sort.

"The dry-cleaning guy had to go liquid. You can imagine I drove a bargain."

Again, Remmie nodded. "So, you don't read this stuff?"

"Oh, I pick a magazine up now and again. Maybe one of the romance novels, for shits and giggles is all. But that's not why we're here, now is it?" Flaco drank from his glass, poured another shot. He shifted from gulps to sips. "We're here because you got mixed up with some cartel men from—"

"That's not true. I told you. I came down here to find a girl."

"Right," Flaco said and laughed. "The damsel in distress. How archetypal of you, brother-man. Do your loins clench at the thought of bedding her?"

"What?"

"A hard-on," Flaco said and grinned. "Do you get one when you look at her picture?"

Remmie didn't answer.

Flaco raised his glass in a toast. "You also mentioned some money."

"I did."

"No small amount."

"It isn't a fortune," Remmie said.

"It's a sum that, for the right amount of effort, makes a tasty treat."

Remmie sipped from his tequila glass. The liquid burned his lips and throat. "You want some of the money." Remmie knew this shouldn't surprise him. He wanted to choke himself for revealing too much information to a person he'd only met a few hours previous.

Flaco shook his head and said, "No, I want all the money.

All of it."

"What if she spent it?"

"All of it? The whole grip?"

Remmie said, "It's possible."

"No," Flaco said, "it's not. Especially when a few pesos gets you a decent meal and a drunk afternoon's worth of margaritas."

"I think a woman like Veranda might take a stronger drink than a margarita."

Flaco sipped his tequila and stared at Remmie.

There was a threatening manner to the folds of Flaco's face, an anger hinting at the corners of his mouth and eyes. His hair shone stark white against the house's cool darkness. He crossed one leg over the other, wagged a sandaled foot at Remmie.

Remmie shrugged. "I'm not going to say she spent it all, but what if she did?"

"She didn't."

"If?"

"Then you got yourself some free help from a clever fixer, name of Flaco."

Remmie leaned back into the couch, let his ribs collapse on his lungs and other organs. He grunted with the pain. All he wanted to do was find Veranda Cline and be done with this journey. He said, "Your place overlooks Puerto Santo Thomás—that's what you told me. Are you a liar?"

Flaco stood, smoothed down the purple board shorts and lifted a finger to beckon Remmie. "Come on out back, brother-man. Let me show you the million-dollar view."

● ● ●

From Flaco's rotted wood balcony, Puerto Santo Thomás looked humble and forlorn one hundred feet below them, a ramshackle assemblage of shacks in semi-circle beside an inlet. Open bow fishing boats—the kind with outboard motors steered by hand—bobbed next to anchored buoys. Remmie lifted a hand to his forehead, tried to look for a shiny white car gleaming in the mid-afternoon sun. After staring for a few minutes, he said, "I don't see the car. You think I'd be able to see it?"

Flaco shrugged. He still carried his shot glass full of tequila in one hand, the thin-blown glass pinched between thumb and forefinger. "She could have ditched the car."

"I would have."

Flaco said, "If she was smart, she sold it. Lots of chop shops from here on up to Tijuana."

"I suppose she'd be comfortable around people like that."

"If she's comfortable around people like that...I hate to tell you this, Remmie Miken." Flaco paused and finished his tequila, smacked his lips together and yawned. "If she's comfortable around people like that, then she is people like that."

"Nobody said she was perfect."

"No," Flaco said, "Nobody did. And if they had, they'd be a liar."

28

THE ROAD INTO PUERTO SANTO THOMÁS was a rocky dirt lane. It ran for a mile or two along a ridgeback spine of cliffs above the sea. Flaco, one-handed, slid and whipped the Volkswagen along the road. Remmie swayed in the passenger seat. It hurt him to brace against the car's movement, so he let himself swing back and forth like a crash test dummy. Through the windshield, he watched whitewash from large waves spray foam along the distant curves. He was surprised to find himself here. He was about to do what Trevor Spends planned, and Remmie didn't expect to get paid. Leo Action might be after him (and had been after Trevor, now dead with a capital D), a drug cartel wanted Remmie out of Mexico, and for him to deliver a message to Leo Action, and Flaco—the wily old bastard—planned to take any money Veranda Cline happened to be carrying.

Still, Remmie wanted to see the woman; this was his final and prominent goal.

"Hell of a road," Remmie said.

"Well, these folks don't much care for outsiders."

"Not friendly to gringos, huh?"

Flaco grunted. "The thing about Mexico, it's paradise for the right kind of person. But for anybody else, well, it's just the darkest place they've ever been. Hell, ever will go."

"I happen to think it's alright." Remmie rubbed his sore abdomen, flinched. He sensed Flaco's eyes on him, wished the man would watch the road and nothing else.

"Those aches and pains are nothing, Remmie. That's just the kid stuff."

"I got a couple dead friends, too."

"Yeah," Flaco said, "But you still got the 'it can't happen to me' look."

"What makes you say that?"

Flaco took the next turn too fast and the car's rear tires slid, neared the cliff's edge. The engine groaned and the tires gained purchase. They resumed their trajectory toward the fishing village. "I'll tell you what makes me say that," Flaco said. He checked his rearview mirror, shook his head, and said, "You're still here, that's what. You haven't given up, and that means you haven't learned your lesson. Believe me, I've seen it before—things aren't what you want, Remmie."

"You don't know what I want."

"Sure I do. You want what everybody wants: A good woman. Money. Paradise lost."

Remmie didn't reply to that. He stared out the windshield as the road unfurled. He felt his breath quicken and, when it did, he reached out and planted his hands on the car's dash. All at once, Remmie Miken was bracing himself; he didn't know what was coming next.

● ● ●

Puerto Santo Thomás smelled to Remmie like day old fish guts, a little ocean salt thrown in for seasoning. The village was perched on the wind-protected side of a small inlet. Fishing shacks—he couldn't call them anything else—were stacked atop and alongside each other. Flaco pulled the car along the slightly paved road. It ran behind the village, along a brick wall holding back about ten thousand tons of Baja desert. Beyond the fisherman's homes—many decorated with cast-offs from the sea, old buoys and bottles, rusted anchors, battered wooden pieces of broken apart vessels—a beige, church-like building leered at them from a hill; all of this nestled against the sea like some crooked postcard image.

The car slid along the road, beneath a gate with a copper bell atop its center, stopped.

Flaco shut off the engine, set the parking brake, and sighed. "If she hasn't seen us by now, she's dumb as a sea cucumber. Chances are, she's thinking about how to get away right this minute."

"Maybe." Remmie wasn't sure. He watched the courtyard in front of the church-like building. No movement. There were no lights in the windows either. "What the hell is this place?"

"Resort, or it used to be. Somewhat heavy use in the summer. Looks like nobody's home."

"That's what I was thinking."

Flaco yawned and said, "Looks like. Why don't you ring the bell?"

Remmie got out of the car, walked back to the gate with the bell high above him. It swayed in the ocean breeze. A salt-crusted rope ran down from the bell, stopped at about head high. Remmie reached up and yanked. The bell clanged three times, echoed into the village.

The sound died and all Remmie was left with was the slushing sound of the sea and one lone caw from a seagull. He listened for footsteps. None came. He reached up and yanked the rope again—clang-clang-clang sounded amidst the ocean waves. He looked back at Flaco in the driver's seat. The man's hard, angry-inquisitive eyes reflected in the rear-view mirror. His look gave nothing away. Remmie scanned the courtyard. For a few more minutes, there was nothing. Remmie began to think that Veranda Cline was gone. He imagined, somehow, she hopped a ferry to the mainland, caught a bus in Mexico City. Best he figured, she was probably three sheets to the wind on some Brazilian beach by now. But then he heard a voice:

"Hola, amigo."

Remmie turned and saw a young man with slicked down hair descend a nearby stairway. He wore clean Levis, a button-down shirt, and scuffed cowboy boots. Behind him, a young woman held a baby wrapped in a blue blanket. She bounced the baby on a hip and stared without blinking.

"You want a camping spot?" The young man spoke good English.

Remmie shook his head. "No, señor. Gracias. I'm looking for somebody—a woman."

The young man reached Remmie, but averted his eyes. Instead, he stared out to sea, watched the sun sink into throbbing blue. After a few seconds, he shook his head.

Remmie kept at it. "An American woman. Young. She's pretty, too." He looked for a second at the woman on the staircase. "Like your wife."

This got the young man's attention. His eyes burned into Remmie's. "I never seen another woman around here, not since the spring. Maybe a grandma or two, for the fisherman. No beautiful women. Believe me, I tell you if I do." He motioned at the fishing shacks. "We all talk about it."

"So if I start banging on doors, I'm not going to hear about a woman in a nice American car, am I? Look, como se llama, amigo?"

The young man smirked and said, "Rodrigo. I own the hotel. My tio, he gave it to me."

Remmie looked casually at the hotel, tilted his head as if to dismiss it. "Shit, I wish I had me a rich uncle. I could sure use a hotel. Especially so I can put up a pretty lady from—"

"I told you," Rodrigo said. "It's me, my wife, my baby. ¿Sabes?"

Remmie chanced another look at the staircase, noticed the man's wife was gone. He looked back at the Baja Bug, noticed Flaco climbing out of the car. He slammed the door and began to walk toward Remmie. Back to the young Mexican now, and Remmie noticed the guy was looking over his shoulder. He heard the Dodge Charger before he saw it—a throaty purr against the hushing sound of the ocean. The sound increased in volume as the car reached the far wall running alongside the west end of the hotel. The Charger's white nose—sleek, aerodynamic bumper and partial hood—peeked out from behind the wall, stopped, shot forward in a rush of sound. The car spun counter-clockwise, centered on the three men—Flaco, Remmie, the Mexican hotel man named Rodrigo—and began to creep forward. The windshield was tinted too dark to see the driver.

Remmie said, "It's her."

"She paid me," Rodrigo said. "She drive me crazy. Loco, gringo."

Remmie gulped, tensed up with the fight or flight adrenaline he'd felt so often these last two days. "The hell is she going to do now?"

Flaco held out one hand like a traffic cop marching

around some nameless American city.

The Dodge Charger roared. The tires shot dust and the car—my, it happened fast—came at them like some insane creature of machinery and guts.

All three men screamed.

• • •

Remmie rolled to his left, away from Rodrigo, and hit the dirt hard on elbows and knees. Blood ran down his forearms, left dark spots on the dirt. The Dodge Charger—likely driven by Veranda Cline—missed Rodrigo and Flaco, too. Both men were up, dusting themselves off, while Remmie watched Veranda speed out of the village, steer the car onto the curvy, cliff-top road. He was back at the Volkswagen in seconds. "Hurry the fuck up. Let's go." Remmie slapped the top of the car, slid into the passenger seat. He made sure to buckle his seatbelt.

Flaco slid in next to him and said, "The bitch is crazy, and she better have the money."

"I wouldn't spend it before you get it."

Flaco glared at Remmie, fired up the car. He spun them around like a stunt driver, shot them past the ramshackle dwellings. They hit the first curve too fast and a front tire caught rocks on the roadside, made Flaco slow for an instant to regain control. He righted the steering and punched the accelerator. The engine whined like a fat cat in an alley fight.

Before them, a dust cloud rose into the sky.

"That's her. Fucking punch it."

"No shit," Flaco said. "She doesn't know this road like I do."

Soon, Remmie caught the white, ass-end of the Charger swinging back and forth through curves. The tail lights didn't light up at all—Veranda drove with all throttle. Like the bad ass she was for running from Trevor Spends, from Leo Action, from her fucking parents.

"This bitch better take it slow, or she'll end up in hell."

Remmie said, "I doubt she gives two shits about death."

The Volkswagen's suspension creaked as they rounded the next curve, power slid into a long straight; the road traced a cliff's edge above the sea and Remmie found his ass clenching as he looked over the side. Heading into town was easier. He didn't see the drop off. Looking at it now, he shivered. "Stay to the left, man. Last thing I want is a saltwater bath."

Flaco grimaced, gripped the wheel with both hands. His white hair flared out behind him. "Let me tell you something, gringo-ass-motherfucker. I've been driving roads in Baja since Reagan got jerked off by the American public. Shit, I got more miles on these roads than your little lady up there has on her smooth precious landing path. You want me to catch her, hold onto your goddamn junk." Flaco's head jerked violently, like a puppet caught in odd stage light. In an absent-minded tone, as if he didn't mean for Remmie to hear, Flaco said, "God, I want that money."

They rounded another curve. Remmie caught the badland textures of desert flashing in the windshield; scrub bush and cacti, brown soil and fool's gold flaking through granite.

He tightened his seatbelt.

He thought back to the image on Trevor's cell phone: He saw Veranda in his mind, this young looker with too little time in her pretty green eyes. Why did all the world have to shoot hell right through you? In his belly, Remmie noticed a squeezing; it wasn't his ribs or the pain from eating too little. No, it was the nervous certainty that his plans—as ass-backward as they were—were about to get scrambled. And then he told himself: You never had plans, Remmie. Shit, you never have. Your whole life has been one meaningless fucking plot point after another. The farthest you plan is the next sip of whiskey, the next can of beer, the next second in a long line of French fry minutes.

Remmie, you're a broke-ass fry cook about to eat dust in Baja.

He shook his head. No. No. No. And then Remmie began to scream the word: "No! No! No! Fuck no! Veranda! Fuck you! No, Veranda! Fucking no, Veranda!"

"What the shit is wrong with you now?" Flaco took his eyes off the road, put them on Remmie. "You're going nuts too, now. I thought you had some sane in you, brother-man. I thought—" Flaco's mouth clenched as he steered the Volkswagen around a treacherous curve.

No. No. No. It stopped coming from Remmie's mouth, but it ran through his blood stream, circulated like a mantra in his head, a chorus he couldn't shake. He was seeing the future before it unfolded. But now, with the word etching through him, he saw everything in real time: Ahead of them, where the road curled westward before finally turning east, the white ass of the Dodge Charger lit up—for the first time—with the red glow of tail lights.

Remmie saw the license plate through the dust, a senseless mix of numbers and letters.

Like his life. Like every life.

And, as if in slow motion, Remmie saw Veranda Cline drive over the edge.

29

A SURREAL SIGHT LAY BEFORE REMMIE. Down on the beach, in the smooth gold sands where azure waters washed up and back like God's saliva, a white Dodge Charger, part-crushed, jutted from the sands. The front half of the car was mangled, hundreds of shattered windshield pieces dotted the sand, reflected the gray-blue sky. Veranda Cline—Remmie figured it was her—was motionless in the sand, about thirty feet from the vehicle—ejected through the windshield. She wore a white tank-top and short Levi shorts, cut off at mid-thigh. Her feet were bare. The beach was empty save for the car and the woman and one other body—Veranda's dead brother. The dead detective was bound in clear plastic, propped there in the sand like cast off trash, his bearded face partly visible. He lay closer to the car, and the whitewash from the sea brushed over him like a cloud, washed away. Remmie squinted at Veranda and thought he could see blood on her face, growing in shades across her abdomen. The sun was low in the west, but still not touching the swelling horizon of the sea. Remmie knew this: He'd have to go down there and look at her, make sure it was real—make sure that his chance at love was dead. One part of him grieved at losing something he'd never held, but another part of him clammed up, clenched like the twisted skin of a weary and ancient scar.

Flaco moved beside him and said, "Holy shit. The money is…"

Remmie saw where Flaco's eyes settled; a few feet beyond Veranda's motionless body, a black duffel bag floated in the sea, moved in and out with the wash of waves. Surrounding it were leaflets of dark green paper—all the money.

Flaco cursed again, started to negotiate the crumbling cliffside. A thin path ran to their left, wound through small shrubs toward the sands below. He almost ran, but caught himself as rocks slid from beneath his feet, fell off the cliff and landed near the mangled car.

Remmie watched as Flaco, a skinny American with floppy white hair, traversed the cliff, reached the sand, and sprinted toward the water. He fell into the waves, flailed wildly after the duffel bag. The waves—somehow—kept tugging the bag and the loose money farther out to sea. Flaco screamed like a mad man—no matter how hard he flailed or kicked, the money and bag slid toward the horizon. After what seemed a long time, Flaco stopped swimming and simply floated atop the waves, bobbed like a seabird. When the sun touch the sea, Flaco turned and swam back to shore.

Remmie started down the cliffside. He wanted to see Veranda Cline.

Even if she was dead.

● ● ●

Veranda Cline looked the same as she did in the image on

Trevor's phone, if a little more plump around the face. Her eyes, still almond shaped and deep green, were fixed on the darkening sky. Her skin—her thighs and ankles and breasts—were cold to the touch. Remmie clenched one of her hands in his own, pinched the cold tip of her index finger. Looking down on her from high atop the cliff, he'd felt grief, or a kind of grief. But now, here beside her, he felt nothing. He felt vacant.

Like he had in the church.

Like he had his entire life.

All this, the entire journey, ended in absence. It ended in death. Remmie stood and shook his head at the woman's lifeless body. All his journey, if it had been for Veranda Cline, had been for nothing. The money, too, had washed out to sea like so much garbage. In his head, Remmie called himself a fool, a seeker of nothing. He was always and forever headed downward, toward the nothingness below his feet. He remembered something his ex-wife once told him: Consider yourself lucky, Remmie Miken. After all, you're the sucker.

And only one of those is born each day.

Sucker. A seeker of nothing.

Flaco emerged from the water. He shivered in the cold and hopped from one foot to the other. "Need to get us a boat," he said. "Someone must have a kayak around here. A dinghy. Hell, a damn trash can lid that floats. Whatever works. That's a shit-ton of money out there."

"It's gone," Remmie said.

"The hell it is."

Remmie looked again at Veranda and tried to memorize her. Memorize the dead, he implored himself. When the image was burned in his head and etched across his heart, he looked at Flaco. "You're going to end up with nothing."

"Shit, brother-man. We all do. Just a deep hole and a few halfway decent hand jobs. That's the best we can ask for. A bit of money never hurt a man though. And I'll tell you—"

Remmie turned and Flaco's voice was lost on the wind. He never heard the skinny man's voice again. Remmie started up the cliffside trail without turning back, pushed himself until his thighs screamed with pain and his ribs throbbed. When he reached the top, he was short of breath and his heart felt like a piston firing in his throat. Still, he didn't stop—Remmie got inside the Volkswagen on the driver's side. He turned the key and fired the engine.

He looked once more over the cliff, drank in the blue mass of ocean and dark sky.

Remmie shifted the Volkswagen into gear and started east down the dirt road.

30

IT WASN'T LONG BEFORE REMMIE saw the paved highway in the distance. He guessed it wasn't so long a trip when you weren't being shoved in the mud and threatened by cartel men. And it wasn't so long either if you weren't chasing some crazy woman who found the guts to raise her middle finger at a small-time gangster.

When you're driving for the hell of it, every road is short.

He rounded a bend and saw the husk of Trevor's burned out Mustang. Remmie slowed the Volkswagen and scanned the Mustang's surroundings for anything of value. Nothing but scraps of rubber. Sad, to see an American car waylaid on some dusty road in deepest Mexico. Sad, indeed. Remmie shrugged and floored the engine; the tires caught pavement and he turned south.

As the night crawled in and headlights flitted past him heading the opposite direction, Remmie caught a brief moment of clarity. It wasn't the end, he figured. Because the end never really mattered: The money. Veranda. The Dodge Charger. Nope—it was none of that. It was the journey, the dusty, rubber-trodden road and all its highwaymen.

The journey, he realized, was everything.

The Volkswagen thrummed down the highway, took the curves with loose abandon, rattled toward Mulegé, Santa Rosalia, La Paz and Cabo San Lucas.

All points south.

There were more roads Remmie could travel; some of these roads—in disrepair—were on the map, but others, he knew, were uncharted. Yes, Remmie needed more roads.

And, God willing or not, he would find them.

After many miles staring hard into the darkness, Remmie checked his rearview mirror. There were no headlights, but he saw something there, vague shadows in his head. He saw Big Arms with his automatic rifle, all his cartel men piled in a pickup truck, their shirts and hair waving frantically as they pursued a poor American in an unproven Volkswagen. Behind them, in a black Crown Vic (or something like it), Remmie saw Leo Action, his plump face terse and determined in the night. He saw Rico Castillas, too. And his compadres.

Remmie saw all the ghosts of his life. And they pursued him.

He pulled his eyes from the mirror and looked back through his windshield at the unfolding countryside. More checkpoints, he wondered?

Remmie saw again the hard Mexican Marine from outside Ensenada. He imagined those dark, knowing eyes boring into him, prying at him like leeches.

And in the deepest parts of his consciousness, in a cold dark place with no name, Remmie heard a sound: The sure-fire click of a bullet chambered, readied...fired.

And it was for him.

ACKNOWLEDGMENTS

I'd like to thank my wife Lesley for her constant support, understanding, and joy. You are a wonderful mother and wife. I love you so much. I'd like to thank my son, Charlie Paul, for always making me laugh. I love you, man! I have to thank Ron Earl at Shotgun Honey and the folks at Down & Out Books; all your hard work is appreciated. Thanks to you all. And, lastly, I want to thank YOU for reading this book. Thank you for buying independent, for reading this odd story, and for listening to the sound of my voice. Let's all keep telling tales...

MATT PHILLIPS lives in San Diego. His books include ***Know Me from Smoke***, ***Accidental Outlaws***, and ***Three Kinds of Fool***. More info at www.MattPhillipsWriter.com

DOWN & OUT BOOKS

On the following pages are a few
more great titles from the
Down & Out Books publishing family.

For a complete list of books and to
sign up for our newsletter,
go to **DownAndOutBooks.com**.

SHOTGUN HONEY

ABC
GROUP DOCUMENTATION

ALL DUE RESPECT

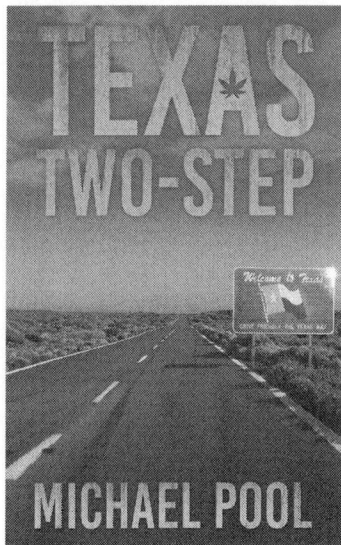

Texas Two-Step
A Russ Kirkpatrick Novel
Michael Pool

Down & Out Books
April 2018
978-1-946502-56-8

Cooper and Davis are a couple of Widespread Panic-obsessed Texas ex-pats growing some of Denver's finest organic cannabis. At least they were, until legal weed put the squeeze on their market. When their last out-of-state dealer gets busted, they're left with no choice but to turn to their reckless former associate Sancho Watts to unload one last crop in Teller County, Texas.

What ensues is an East Texas criminal jamboree with everyone involved keeping their cards so close to their vest that all the high-stakes dancing around each other is sure to result in bloodshed.

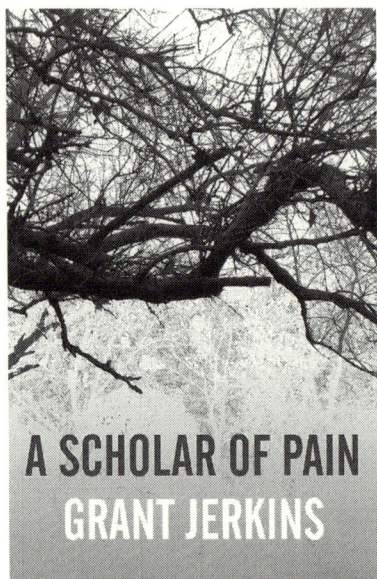

A Scholar of Pain
Grant Jerkins

ABC Group Documentation
an imprint of Down & Out Books
February 2018
978-1-946502-15-5

In his debut short fiction collection, Grant Jerkins remains—as the Washington Post put it—"Determined to peer into the darkness and tell us exactly what he sees." Here, the depth of that darkness is on evident, oftentimes poetic, display. Read all sixteen of these deviant diversions. Peer into the darkness.

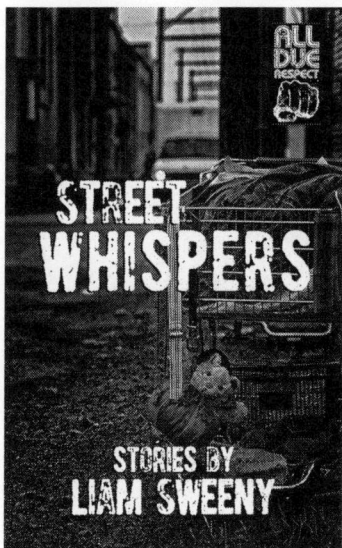

Street Whispers
Stories by Liam Sweeny

All Due Respect
an imprint of Down & Out Books
February 2018
978-1-946502-86-5

An eclectic collection of pulp, grit and noir stories inspired by the Capital Region of New York, a rust-belt crossroads in the shadow of the city that never sleeps.

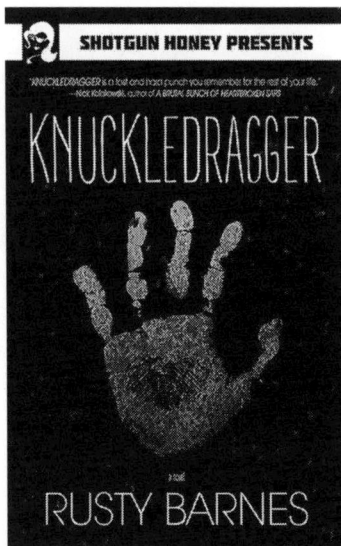

Knuckledragger
Rusty Barnes

Shotgun Honey
an imprint of Down & Out Books
October 2017
978-1-946502-07-0

Hooligan and low-level criminal enforcer Jason "Candy" Stahl has made a good life collecting money for his boss Otis. One collection trip, though, at the Diovisalvo Liquor Store, unravels events that turn Candy's life into a horror-show.

In quick succession he moves up a notch in the organization, overseeing a chop shop, while he falls in lust with Otis's girlfriend Nina, gets beaten for insubordination, and is forced to run when Otis finds out about Candy and Nina's affair.

Made in the USA
Middletown, DE
26 June 2019